sew zoey

BURSTING AT THE seams

written by
Chloe Taylor

illustrated by
Nancy Zhang

Simon Spotlight
New York London Toronto Sydney New Delhi

SIMON SPOTLIGHT
An imprint of Simon & Schuster Children's Publishing Division
1230 Avenue of the Americas, New York, New York 10020
First Simon Spotlight paperback edition December 2014
Copyright © 2014 by Simon & Schuster, Inc.
All rights reserved, including the right of reproduction in whole or in part in any form.
SIMON SPOTLIGHT and colophon are registered trademarks of Simon & Schuster, Inc.
For information about special discounts for bulk purchases, please contact Simon & Schuster Special Sales at 1-866-506-1949 or business@simonandschuster.com.
Text by Caroline Hickey
Designed by Laura Roode
Manufactured in the United States of America 1114 OFF
10 9 8 7 6 5 4 3 2 1
ISBN 978-1-4814-1965-9 (hc)
ISBN 978-1-4814-1964-2 (pbk)
ISBN 978-1-4814-1966-6 (eBook)
Library of Congress Catalog Card Number 2014942151

------- CHAPTER 1 ---------

Runway Ready!

Hello, readers!! So, remember when the dress I designed for Bryn Allen was on the cover of *Celebrity* magazine? I do! In fact, it's hard to forget. Since then, I've been getting some e-mails and requests through my Sew Zoey store for more runway looks. I'm not sure that's my speed, exactly, but here's a design that could look great on someone young, without showing too much. The problem is that making it would probably take me thirty or forty hours, which is a *lot* for one dress! I'd need a nice, long vacation afterward. ☺

And speaking of vacations . . . my most favorite aunt, Lulu, is finally back in town after a romantic Caribbean getaway with her (dum dee dum) new fiancé! She and John got engaged while they were on their trip. I'm meeting her for tea and cupcakes after school to get all the juicy details. I'm SEW pumped to see her!

Zoey Webber was in heaven. She was at her favorite café, Tea Time, with a cup of oolong tea, a pink frosted cupcake, and her aunt Lulu. Lulu was tanned and smiling as she drizzled honey into her English breakfast tea and stirred it with a spoon.

"Tell me *everything*," Zoey said. "Don't leave anything out! I want to feel like I was there too!"

Lulu laughed, and began to unwrap the bag that held her croissant. "Well, it *was* pretty magical. Everything about Barbados is magical, really. John and I were out to dinner at a beautiful restaurant built on a cliff at the edge of the ocean. We were watching tiny nurse sharks swim up for chum the restaurant throws them, and when I looked away from the sharks, John was kneeling beside me."

"And?" urged Zoey. She was so enthralled with the story, she hadn't even touched her tea or her cupcake yet. "Did you say yes immediately, or did you cry, or what?"

Lulu laughed again. "Let's just say my eyes were teary, but I was so happy. And I said yes right away. I think I *might* have even shouted it. The people sitting at tables around us applauded, and that was it."

"Sounds *perfect*." Zoey sighed with satisfaction. The story was exactly what she would have wished for her aunt, who had always been more of a second mother to Zoey since her own mom had passed away when she was very little. Although it had been somewhat hard for Zoey when Lulu and John had first begun dating, because she'd been worried she'd lose *her* special place in Lulu's life, that hadn't happened at all. Zoey felt sure that adding John

Chadden to their family would make things even better.

With the proposal story out of the way, Zoey bit into her cupcake with enthusiasm. It was Friday afternoon, and a long and busy week at school had made her ravenous. She was so intent on her cupcake, in fact, that she didn't notice Lulu wasn't touching her own croissant.

When Zoey finally looked up, Lulu was leaning forward in her seat, her eyes bright and her lips clamped together. A smile tugged at the corners of her mouth.

"What is it?" Zoey asked. "Why are you looking at me like that?" Self-conscious, Zoey wiped at her mouth with a napkin, in case she was covered in extra frosting.

"There's a *tiny* bit more to the story . . . ," Lulu said. She giggled and then clapped a hand over her mouth to stop. "But before I tell you, you have to *swear* to keep it a secret."

Zoey felt her heart begin to pound. More to the story? Like what? Her aunt was acting very strangely, and not at all like the calm, cool interior designer and business owner that she was.

"Tell me!" Zoey exclaimed.

Lulu placed her hands on either side of the café table, as if to anchor herself so she wouldn't fall over, and whispered, "John and I are having a surprise wedding, and it's in three weeks!"

Zoey stared at her aunt, her mouth hanging open. A *surprise* wedding? What on Earth was that? In three *weeks*?

Zoey shook her head, unable to spit out a sentence. All she could mumble was *"What?"*

Aunt Lulu giggled again, her sparkling eyes and flushed cheeks making her look every bit the happy and excited bride-to-be. "We've decided to invite our close friends and family to a little 'engagement party' at my house in a few weeks. At least, that's what they'll think. But when everyone arrives, we're really going to surprise them and tell them we'll be getting married that night!"

Zoey had never heard of a surprise wedding. "So the wedding, the *actual* wedding where you say your vows, is in *three weeks* at your house, but no one will know except you and John and me?"

Lulu nodded. "And a few other close family members, like your dad and brother. And the vendors. We'll have a caterer and a cake and flowers and a photographer, like a normal wedding. But it'll all just be a little more casual and fun, since it'll be at my house and no one will expect it."

Zoey's mind reeled with the possibilities. No church, no big reception hall. No waiting months and months for the big day. A surprise wedding for her aunt, in just three weeks. And she was one of the few in on the secret!

"I LOVE IT!" Zoey screeched, and several people in the café turned to glance at her. Lulu and Zoey looked at each other and grinned. "I really do, Aunt Lulu. This is so *you*."

Lulu winked at her. "Exactly. John and I have both been married before, and we didn't want to do the big wedding thing again. We love each other, and we want to start our life together *now*. And the surprise just makes it so much more fun!" She paused, taking a sip of her tea and then carefully placing the teacup back on its saucer. "And there's something very special I'd like to ask you, Zoey."

"I'm not sure I can take any more exciting news, Aunt Lulu," Zoey said honestly. "I'm already on a sugar high from the cupcake, and now I know the biggest secret ever!"

Aunt Lulu put her hand over Zoey's and squeezed it. "I'd like you to be my junior bridesmaid, honey. And I'd really love it if you'd come shopping with me and help me pick out my dress."

Zoey was honored. Truly honored. She'd get to stand up with her aunt at the wedding *and* help find the dress. It was a dream come true!

"Of course, yes to both!" Zoey said. "I can't wait!"

"My maid of honor will be my best friend, Sybil, but since she lives in Atlanta, she won't be here to shop with me. I'd like for you and her to wear dresses that coordinate, at least in color. She'll buy hers, but I think it would be wonderful if you designed and made your own junior bridesmaid's dress."

Design my own junior bridesmaid's dress? Zoey was flabbergasted. With that final piece of exciting news, Zoey jumped up from her seat and threw her arms around her aunt. What could be more fun?

She'd make the most beautiful junior bridesmaid's dress in the world!

Aunt Lulu hugged Zoey back, smoothing Zoey's hair with one hand. "I take it that's a yes?"

Zoey nodded and gave her aunt one more big squeeze before returning to her seat. A really good afternoon for Zoey was a cupcake and conversation with her aunt. Hearing about a wedding proposal made it extra special. Finding out about a secret wedding made it unbelievable. Hearing that she'd be a junior bridesmaid *and* get to design her own dress? Zoey didn't have a word for it.

"I think I might burst," she told Lulu. "I think I'm going to burst right through the walls of Tea Time."

Lulu chuckled. "Well, if possible, *don't*. And remember, the only people you can discuss this with are Marcus and your father. We have to keep it a secret so that the surprise works. It's very important to John and me. Promise?"

Zoey nodded. "I promise," she said.

She had no idea how difficult that promise would be to keep.

✦

The next morning, Lulu picked up Zoey, and they drove to a fancy bridal salon. Zoey had never been wedding dress shopping before, and she couldn't even remember the last wedding she'd attended. Probably her cousin's wedding when Zoey was about seven. She had no idea what to expect when they walked in.

A chic, middle-aged woman in a fitted black suit approached them. "Good morning. Do you have an appointment?" she asked.

"Yes, I'm Lulu Price," Aunt Lulu said.

The woman checked a clipboard, nodded, and ushered them back to a large round room, with racks and racks of gorgeous dresses on display, and a wall of dressing rooms on one side.

The consultant, Deirdre, gave Lulu a quick tour of the gowns, showing her how they were grouped by price. "And when is your wedding?" Deirdre asked, making notes on her clipboard.

With slightly pink cheeks, Lulu explained she was having a surprise wedding at her house in just three weeks, and she wanted something not too formal, but elegant, and that it needed to be ready to purchase and alter immediately.

"Three weeks?" Deirdre repeated. "*Three weeks?*"

Zoey's eyes swiveled from Lulu to Deirdre and back to Lulu. What was the big deal about three weeks?

Lulu simply nodded, and said firmly, "Yes, three weeks. What do you have that's ready to wear?"

Deirdre wrinkled her brow a moment, and looked worried, but then her face seemed to relax. "I love a challenge," she told Lulu. "Go into the dressing room, please, and I'll bring you some sample dresses available for purchase, and also a few of our consignment dresses. They can all go home with you immediately."

Lulu sighed with relief, and she and Zoey headed to the dressing room.

Zoey whispered to her aunt, "I didn't realize you couldn't buy a wedding dress off the rack," she said. "What's the big deal?"

Lulu explained. "Most wedding dresses are made to order. So you go to a bridal store, try on a sample, and then they order it in your size. When it comes in, which can take months, you usually have to alter it some. That's what happened with my first wedding. But we don't have time for that now, so I'll just have to take what I can get."

Zoey sat, slightly worried. She wanted her aunt to have the perfect dress. She didn't want her to have to settle for whatever samples or consignment dresses were available that very second.

Deirdre knocked and came into the dressing room, her arms full of gowns. They were beautiful, every one of them, and varied from silk chiffon to tulle to lace.

Aunt Lulu began trying them on. Luckily, she wore a standard dress size, and was able to fit into most of the samples. The first dress, a strapless silk chiffon with seed pearls and sequins, was too formal for a fall wedding in someone's backyard. The second, a voluminous ball gown, had a skirt so wide, it would never fit through the front door of Lulu's house. The third was a possibility, with wide straps, a square décolletage, and a smooth flowy skirt. It wasn't too formal, and it looked appropriate for a surprise wedding at home. But, unfortunately, Lulu was a bit on the tall side, and the dress was three inches too short, even without heels, and the hem wasn't quite long enough to let down.

"There's no fixing a too-short dress," Lulu said with a groan. "Too long would have been a better problem."

"You could cut it and make it knee-length?" Zoey suggested. She was starting to feel discouraged by Lulu's limited options.

"I really want a long dress," Lulu said. "In fact, I really like the *top* of this dress, but with the *bottom* of that first one. It's too bad it's not like magnetic dress-up dolls where you can mix and match!"

Lulu tried on several more dresses, but none of them were right either. Everything was either too formal or fit poorly. Finally, she looked at Zoey, and blinked. "I think we've struck out," she said dejectedly.

Zoey's mind raced. They had to find a dress for Lulu. They had to!

"What if . . . ," Zoey began, an idea forming in her mind. "What if I were to sketch the top of the dress you liked, with the bottom of that other one, and you gave the sketch to a wedding seamstress and they made it for you? Could that work?"

"It's a terrific idea, Zoey," said Lulu. "But I'm afraid I tried that first! I called my regular seamstress as soon as we got back from Barbados, but she was booked solid. She even gave me some other people to try, but none of them had availability to make a dress so fast. That's why I thought I'd make do with a sample dress."

Deirdre knocked on the dressing room door, and Lulu opened it. "I'm afraid that's all we have available in your size that could be ready in time," Deirdre said. "I'm so terribly sorry! I can call you if we get any new consignment gowns in this week or next."

"Thank you," Lulu said. "Something will work out, I'm sure. I can always look online."

Deirdre removed the dresses, and Lulu put her regular clothes back on. She and Zoey left the store, packed with beautiful wedding gowns that wouldn't be ready in time for Lulu's big day.

"What are you going to do?" Zoey asked her aunt.

Lulu stopped walking and turned to Zoey. "Zoey," she said, "I know this is a lot to ask, especially with you being so busy with school, but is there any way you'd have time to make a dress for me? We could keep the design really simple, but it's the only way I can get what I want in time for the wedding! And it would mean so much to me to wear an original Sew Zoey dress on my wedding day."

Zoey couldn't believe her ears. Her aunt wanted her to make her *wedding* dress? The most important dress of her life?

"But, Aunt Lulu, I don't know *anything* about wedding dresses! I didn't even know you had to order them! I wouldn't know where to start."

"We'll design it together. Just think of it as a simple white dress. And you know a lot more than you think you do, my talented niece. Wasn't an outfit you made just on the cover of *Celebrity* magazine?"

"Well, yes." Zoey blushed. She was so honored that her aunt would even ask. "I'd *love* to, Aunt Lulu. I'd really, really love to!"

Lulu hugged her and said, "This will be great, Zoey. Really special. It fits our surprise wedding theme, don't you think?"

Zoey agreed. It was sort of perfect.

"Why don't you think about the dresses we liked today and come up with a sketch or two? Something that won't be too hard for you to make so fast. And one more thing: I'll need the skirt fabric to be stretchy if it's fitted, because John and I plan to surprise everyone with a tango for our first dance, since we met in ballroom dance class."

"Okay!" agreed Zoey. "I already have some ideas from what we saw. And I began sketching some designs for my junior bridesmaid's dress last night. Maybe you should take me home now so I can get to work. . . ."

Lulu nodded. "Sure thing. Do you still want to come with me tomorrow for a cupcake tasting, flowers, and stationery?"

"Yes, yes, and yes!" said Zoey. "I don't want to miss *anything*!"

Lulu and Zoey linked arms and then headed for the car. They had a lot of work to do.

CHAPTER 2

Bows and Bridesmaids!

I can't believe this! I really *just. Can't. Believe. It.* As if it weren't exciting enough that my aunt is engaged to a wonderful guy, she's asked me to be a junior bridesmaid *and* to design my own dress for the wedding *and* to make her wedding gown! How did I get so lucky? She's having an engagement party in a few weeks, which will also be so much fun, and my grandparents are coming to town for it. I've totally got weddings on the brain. I keep searching online for wedding ideas, and there are *so* many cute and crafty things you can do!

I've made a few sketches for my junior bridesmaid's dress that I like, but this one is my favorite. What do you think, readers? I get to pick the fabric myself, and then my aunt will have her maid of honor coordinate her dress color. I like not matching perfectly—it's much more modern! I've also made a few attempts at wedding dress sketches, but everything I'm drawing is too poufy for my aunt, who wants to keep things more "elegant chic" than "princess romance." I'll get it right though. . . . I just need some inspiration!

Sunday morning at the Webber house meant one thing—pancake breakfast. Zoey and her older brother, Marcus, took turns each week being in charge of the meal, often slipping in a secret ingredient to keep things interesting. Today was Zoey's turn to make the batter, and as her father was loading up the coffee machine and her brother sat at the kitchen table texting on his phone, she slipped in a few handfuls of tiny marshmallows. Something about their perfect, white fluffiness made her think they were weddingish, and Zoey was in the mood for everything wedding!

When the family sat down to eat, Mr. Webber took one look at the melted white blobs in his pancakes and laughed. "Well, marshmallow pancakes aren't something you see every day now, are they?"

Marcus laughed too, and took a huge bite. "Pretty tasty," he declared. "Nice work, Zo."

Zoey did an exaggerated bow. "Thank you, thank you." She poured syrup onto her stack and picked up her fork to dig in. Zoey loved Sunday mornings.

"What are you up to today, Zoey?" her father asked. He sipped his coffee and leaned back in his chair. "Anything exciting?"

Zoey nodded. "Yes, actually! I'm headed out with Aunt Lulu again to taste cupcakes and choose flowers and stationery for the you-know-what."

The family had already decided with a secret as large as Lulu's, it might be best for them not to ever refer to it directly, in case one of them were to mention it in public or in front of their friends by accident.

"I can't believe the you-know-what is in three weeks. That's crazy!" Marcus shook his head. "I've got to learn 'Here Comes the Sun' before then. And I want to play it perfectly."

Marcus was in a rock band called the Space Invaders. They were good—so good that they'd been accepted at a rock camp over the summer and played at its finale beach concert. Marcus played the drums in the band, but he'd been learning the guitar, and he turned out to have a natural talent for it. Aunt Lulu had asked him to play an acoustic version of "Here Comes the Sun" for her walk down the aisle. Zoey got the feeling Marcus was uncharacteristically nervous about it.

"You'll be great, Marcus," Zoey said encouragingly. "Aunt Lulu wants to keep everything really personal and special. You playing guitar and me making her dress will be perfect!"

Mr. Webber cleared his throat. "I have to say, Zoey, I'm very impressed you'll be making her wedding gown. That's a big job. Plus your own junior bridesmaid's dress."

"I can do it," Zoey said confidently, finishing the last two bites of her breakfast. "We saw a bunch of dresses yesterday, and I did a lot of online research. I have some terrific ideas. We'll get fabric this week, and then I'll be off and running!"

Marcus got up to start clearing the table, and Zoey glanced at the time on his phone. "Uh-oh!" she said. "Speaking of running, I need to hop in the shower and get dressed. Lulu's picking me up in half an hour!"

"We'll clean up," Mr. Webber said. "You go get ready for more preparation for you-know-what."

"Dad, I'm starting to think you just like saying 'you-know-what,'" Zoey teased.

"You-are-right," he replied.

Cupcake tasting was every bit as fun as it sounded. Zoey and Lulu tried all different types of cake and several different frostings before Lulu decided to be somewhat traditional, by going with white cake inside and vanilla butter-cream frosting outside.

The cupcakes would be stacked on a tiered cake stand in the shape of a wedding cake but would be much more fun for the guests than a traditional cake. Zoey saw several displays of the "wedding (cup)cakes" in the window of the gourmet bakery and agreed with her aunt that cupcakes were the way to go for a backyard wedding.

Next, they headed to a florist Lulu often used when she was staging rooms for her clients and needed fresh flowers. After a quick consultation, which included Lulu pulling several magazine ads of bouquets she liked from her purse, the florist and Lulu settled on a scheme that was "modern autumn," with some traditional fall colors, like gold, orange, and red, mixed with bold pinks. The bride's bouquet would be all white, but wrapped in gorgeous gold ribbon, and there would be small bouquets of seasonal flowers placed strategically throughout Lulu's house, including the powder room, and mums lining the front walk up to her house. Zoey and Sybil would get their own bouquets of brightly colored flowers.

Zoey and Lulu left feeling very pleased with

themselves. Two wedding errands down, only a handful more to go! Suddenly, planning a wedding in just a few weeks didn't seem quite so daunting.

"The stationery store is just up the street in the shopping complex," Lulu said. "I know I want an invitation with a photo. I just need to find one that's simple and elegant and goes with our look."

As they pulled into the parking lot, Zoey saw a large bookstore in the same complex and had an idea.

"Aunt Lulu," she said, "would you mind going to the stationery store alone? I've been dying to look through some wedding magazines for ideas for my design, and I'm feeling so inspired from our cupcakes and flowers that I'd love to go into that bookstore now and take tons of notes!"

Aunt Lulu smiled. "Of course! It's never wise to delay a designer when's she's caught the scent. Just make sure your phone is on, and I'll text you when I'm coming to pick you up, all right?"

Zoey agreed, and Aunt Lulu let her out in front of the bookstore. Zoey patted her back pocket to make sure she had her phone and then went inside.

Zoey had been in this bookstore many times, but usually it was to browse the young readers' section or to buy a gift for a friend. She'd never spent much time in the magazine area.

The bridal section was overwhelming. There were magazines for modern brides, traditional brides, local brides, destination brides, home-made "crafty" brides—everything imaginable! Zoey didn't see anything for brides having sur-prise weddings, but then maybe there weren't quite enough of those happening to merit a dedi-cated magazine. Zoey picked out several of the more modern-looking magazines and found a place at a large table nearby, where she spread out with a sketchbook, pencils, and her inspiration magazines. She really wanted to get the design finalized as soon as possible, so she could begin sewing.

After looking through several of the magazines, and comparing them to her initial sketches, Zoey realized she had a problem. She needed to make sure Lulu's gown was a *wedding* gown, and not just a long white dress, but without covering it with *stuff*.

Lulu wasn't into jewel-encrusted bodices, or lots of pearls and sequins, and for many of the dresses in the magazines, that's what designated them as wedding gowns. It wasn't the cut or style at all.

Zoey frowned, stumped. She thought back to the dresses she'd seen the day before at the salon. They had all felt very weddingish, and some had not been overly beaded or encrusted. *Felt*, she thought. *Felt*. They all *felt* weddingish because of the luxurious materials used and how they hung on the body.

That was it! It was the fabric that would make the dress. Even if Zoey designed a relatively simple, square-necked décolletage with a flowy skirt for her aunt, it would be a wedding dress if it was made of the right fabric. Zoey didn't need to worry about the embroidery and beading. She decided to suggest to Lulu that they use a fabric with a gorgeous pearly sheen, because that was not only bridal, but very flattering to her aunt's coloring.

With a sigh of relief, Zoey began refining one of the sketches and was working so hard, she nearly jumped out of her seat when she heard someone nearby say in a loud whisper, "Zoey!"

Alarmed, she looked up, wondering who on Earth was calling her name. Over by the magazine display stood her friend Gabe from school, waving to her.

Zoey smiled with relief. "Hi, Gabe!" she said. "How are you? What are you doing here?"

Gabe came over to the table and sat in the empty chair beside Zoey. "I'm going to a movie later, but I'm early, and I like to come here sometimes and browse the photography books. Most of them are so expensive, I can't afford to buy them."

He glanced at the wedding magazines spread out in front of Zoey and did a double take. "Don't tell me you have big news to share?" he asked, arching his eyebrows in a teasing manner.

"Big news?" Zoey asked. She thought of the surprise wedding. Gabe couldn't know about it; he'd just sat down!

"All the wedding magazines—are you . . . engaged?" he joked.

Zoey laughed with relief. "*No*. Obviously. But my aunt just got engaged, and she's asked me to make her dress, so I thought I'd come in here and do a little research. It's not the kind of design work I usually do, so I want to get it right."

"That's awesome, Zoey! Congratulations. You just keep on doing cooler and cooler stuff, don't you?"

Zoey blushed. Gabe had a way of making her feel like a million bucks. Maybe that's why she'd always considered him a close friend. Recently, she'd started to think it would be nice if Gabe was a bit more than a friend, but of course, as soon as she'd thought that, he'd started dating their school's visiting student from France, Josie.

"Thanks, Gabe," she said. "You're always so—"

But Zoey didn't have time to finish her sentence. Josie appeared behind Gabe, placing a hand on his shoulder and saying, "Voilà! *Je suis içi.*"

"Hi, Josie," Zoey said warmly. "How are you?"

"*Très bien, merçi!* Gabe and I are seeing a movie at the *cinéma* nearby. And I thought if I came early, I might find him here. . . ."

He looked up at Josie, and she winked at him. For a second, Zoey felt a prick of jealousy. They were so cute together, and they knew each other so well that Josie had guessed Gabe would come to the bookstore before the movie. Zoey's jealous pang quickly relaxed into something more comfortable, like a touch of envy, because Josie and Gabe were so well suited. Josie was a really nice girl, after all, and far away from her home outside Paris. Zoey resolved to continue to be friendly and kind to her.

The three of them chatted awhile, until Gabe and Josie had to leave for their movie. Then Zoey got back to work in earnest. With so many projects always going on—like her Sew Zoey online store, designing for celebrity clients, and now, making a wedding dress—it's not like Zoey had time for a boyfriend, anyway! She and Gabe would stay good friends, and she was mostly happy with that.

---------- CHAPTER 3 ----------

Hardworkin' Dresses!

So I'm trying to really study wedding gowns to learn how to make one for my aunt. And there's a *lot* more to it than just picking a design and sewing it up! Wedding dresses generally have more structure in them than regular dresses. Partly because of the length, and because some have trains, and some are A-line or ball gown–shape, but also because they need to be able to be sat in, eaten in, and danced in! I watched a ballroom dancing competition on TV last night to get ideas from dresses that *really* work hard and allow their wearers to move freely. I learned that many have a high hem on one side to allow the legs to move, or lots of crinolines. I don't think my aunt will like either of those on her wedding dress, but they did inspire me to sketch this foxtrot dress. Does anyone know how to foxtrot anymore? It seems like a very funny-looking dance to me! And aren't horses the ones who trot, not foxes?

On Monday morning Zoey was back at school and happy to see her friends. She'd been so busy over the weekend with Lulu's news and helping with wedding errands that Zoey hadn't even had time to run up the street to the house of her best friend Kate Mackey. Her other two best friends, Priti Holbrooke and Libby Quinn, gathered in the hallway with Zoey and Kate to compare stories about their weekends.

"I read your blog, Zoey, so I know all about Lulu's wedding!" Priti shrieked. Priti was always excitable, but happy, romantic things made her *particularly* excitable. "I'm so thrilled that you get to make her dress!"

"*And* be a junior bridesmaid," Libby added. "So much fun."

Zoey filled them in on a few carefully chosen details, so as not to let on about the surprise wedding. The bell rang, and everyone grabbed their backpacks, ready to head off in different directions.

"I can't wait to start our new electives!" Kate declared. "I've always wanted to learn woodshop, and I never thought I'd get the chance right here at school."

Their school, Mapleton Prep, had recently implemented a new electives program, where students were able to choose a special area of study for part of the semester. Kate would be taking industrial arts, Zoey and Priti were taking home economics, and Libby was taking computer science. As the year went on, they'd have the opportunity to try other electives as well.

The bell rang, and the girls went their separate ways, with Zoey and Priti walking together toward the home ec room. Zoey wasn't sure if home ec was a good choice or not, since she already knew how to sew, but she heard it involved cooking and crafts, and she wanted to learn how to make more than pancakes.

"I just looooove baking," Priti said as they walked through the door. "I can't wait to start. I wish we could take electives all day!"

As Zoey and Priti took their seats, their teacher introduced herself.

"Welcome to home ec, students. I'm happy to have you all here. My name is Mrs. Holmes. During the next few weeks, we'll be learning the basics of sewing and cooking. If you have ended up in this class because you didn't get into the elective of your choice . . ." Mrs. Holmes paused as a few boys, who were huddled together to Zoey's left, mumbled and shoved one another. She cleared her throat. "Let me assure you, you *will* need these skills in your life. You might even enjoy yourselves."

Zoey and Priti glanced sideways at each

other and smiled. They knew *they* would enjoy themselves.

A boy named Carter Perry, who played on the school's basketball team and was in the huddle of loud boys, whispered loudly enough to be heard, "*I* heard this class is a great place to meet girls."

All his friends laughed, but Mrs. Holmes just ignored him.

"Simmer down, kids," she said. "Now, our first class project is going to be—aprons! Aprons that we'll be wearing and using throughout the session, particularly when we begin cooking. I have a basic template here for you to use as your pattern, but to make things a little more fun, I'd like you guys to find a way to upgrade your aprons. Make them a little different, a little more interesting or useful. In fact, it's going to be a contest to see who among you can be the most innovative with your pattern or materials."

Zoey started to feel excited then, thinking about all the things she could do with her apron. What fun home ec was going to be! But her excitement was short-lived as one of her grade's meanest girls, Ivy Wallace, along with her friend Bree Sharpe began whispering on the other side of Priti.

Zoey tried to ignore them, but she couldn't help overhearing Ivy say, "Zoey Webber should *not* be in this class. She's, like, a professional sewer or seamstress or whatever. She's just kissing up by taking home ec, and it's not fair to everyone else."

Bree agreed, which she usually did. "Yeah, we should tell the teacher. They should put her in computer science or something."

Mrs. Holmes, who apparently had excellent ears and a low-tolerance for tween griping, said, "I'm well aware that one of your classmates is an excellent seamstress and designer. Zoey Webber has every right to take this class. The judging for the contest will be blind, so I won't know whose apron is whose. It's anyone's game!"

Bree and Ivy crossed their arms over their chests at the same time, looking both peeved and slightly embarrassed that they'd been called out.

Mrs. Holmes continued, "Also, in my classroom I require students to show up ready to learn and to participate with enthusiasm. If you cannot do that, you are free to visit Principal Austen's office. Now, if there will be no more chitchat, I'm going to teach you all how to sew. Let's begin."

I like her! Priti scrawled on a piece of scrap paper, pushing it toward Zoey.

Me too, Zoey wrote back. *Bring on the aprons!*

Mrs. Holmes began demonstrating the basics of threading a needle, making and tying off stitches, and operating a sewing machine. Today, students would just play around with the machines and try to get down the basics. They would start the aprons in the next class. Zoey couldn't help feeling a touch bored as she practiced running a length of scrap fabric through her machine, and she began to daydream about her plans for her aunt's dress.

Suddenly, her machine jammed with the needle stuck in the up position. Zoey, mad at herself for daydreaming when she knew better than to take her eyes off the machine while it was running, tried to get the needle free. But the school machines were very different from Zoey's own machine at home, which had been her mother's and was at least twenty years old. She did have a more modern machine, which she had received as a gift from the Speedman Sewing Machine company, but it always worked perfectly. It looked to Zoey like some internal mechanism on the school machine had jammed, but she couldn't figure out how get it to *un*jammed.

Red-faced, Zoey continued to try and fix the machine, conscious that a few other students nearby had noticed her problem and were probably wondering why the "famous" Sew Zoey was having trouble with a simple piece of scrap fabric. Out of nowhere a tall slender boy, with long bangs that hung in his eyes and a pair of burnt orange corduroys, appeared beside Zoey.

"Can I try?" he asked quietly, motioning at the machine.

Zoey looked up at him, surprised. "*You* can fix this?"

He nodded, a smile pulling up one corner of his mouth. "I've got a similar machine at home," he explained.

Zoey gestured for him to try, and he quickly and deftly began to manipulate the needle and bobbin while holding down a reset button on the side of the machine. It worked. He was able to unlock the needle, and in barely sixty seconds he had the thread untangled and the machine ready to go again.

Zoey was amazed. "How did you do that?" she asked. "I'm usually pretty good with sewing machines."

The boy shrugged. "I told you, I've got a machine like this at home. This brand is very temperamental, but they last forever. That's why they use them in schools. Just be sure to keep your speed on the pedal smooth and consistent. If you get choppy, it'll bind up your thread and lock your needle."

Zoey nodded, still slightly dumbstruck. She was so grateful, she nearly forgot to say thank you. "Th-thank you," she sputtered finally. "I'm Zoey, by the way."

"I know," said the boy. "I'm Sean Waschikowski, master sewing machine fixer, at your service." He gave a small bow and then headed back to his seat.

Mrs. Holmes, who had seen the whole thing, clapped several times, and said, "Thank you to our new resident technician, Sean. Everyone else, please keep practicing. And start thinking about your apron designs. Make yours special! You may end up using it for years and years to come."

Zoey heard Carter make another comment, something about planning to wear his apron to professional sporting events *only*, and Priti nudged her with her elbow.

"Is he for real?" Priti whispered. "Too bad he's so cute," she added, and Zoey smothered a laugh.

Zoey glanced over at Carter. He *was* sort of cute, but obnoxious. "Yuck," she said. "No thank you."

"That Sean guy was really nice," Priti said. "And cute, too. I can't believe there's someone here who knows as much about sewing as you!"

"Me, neither," said Zoey. "I wonder if his sewing is as good as his machine fixing."

"We'll find out," said Priti. "Wouldn't that be interesting?"

"*Very* interesting," said Zoey, who wasn't sure how she felt about how good Sean was with a machine. "I think."

CHAPTER 4

Sew Excited for My New Elective!

After all the sewing I've done, I'm finally taking a real sewing class! It's a home ec elective at my school (which inspired this updated '50s look), and it will include cooking as well, but first we're beginning with a sewing project. We have to make our own aprons, improving the basic pattern in some way. It's a fun idea, and an apron is one thing I've never made! It's hard to believe there's anything I haven't made at this point—I mean, I've made outfits for dogs, hair accessories, screen-printed T-shirts, and soon a junior bridesmaid's dress and a wedding gown!

I just got a few new orders through my Sew Zoey site on Etsy that I need to fill, which means I'll be busy for a while. Plus, all my teachers have decided to give extra homework lately. . . . Eeek! Luckily, Monday evenings are still one of my favorite nights of the week because I get to tap-dance with one of my besties! *Tap, tap, tappity tap!* (PS I am never going to get the hang of the time step. Seriously. It's sooooo hard!)

Mrs. Mackey dropped off Zoey and Kate at tap class Monday evening. Zoey wore a simple black leotard, but over it, she'd added a short wrap skirt she'd made from the custom fabric Daphne Shaw, Zoey's favorite designer and fashion fairy god-mother, had sent her and which were printed with Zoey's sketches. Zoey had used most of the fabric to make pieces of wall art for her friends, and a skirt for Daphne Shaw, but she'd had about two yards leftover and figured it would make a great twirly skirt for tap class. She also wore a pair of brightly colored striped leg warmers. For her, dressing for class was half the fun. The other half was being with Kate.

Kate looked athletic and graceful, as always. She wore a beautiful pale-blue leotard, with a matching chiffon skirt attached, and her long blond hair was plaited on one side of her head. She no longer had to wear her sling and could do small arm movements in class.

"So how was industrial arts?" Zoey asked Kate as the dancers stretched to warm up before class.

"It was so fun!" Kate said. "I really can't wait to start my first project. Today we learned a bunch of safety stuff, like about wearing goggles and how to use the tools and watching out for the people around you. Lorenzo is in my class, and a few other guys from the soccer team, but I don't know the other kids."

Lorenzo Romy was a boy in their grade whom Zoey thought often looked at Kate like he liked her.

She'd never mentioned it to Kate directly, since Kate was decidedly more into sports than boys. But Zoey wouldn't have been at all surprised if Lorenzo had taken the class just because he'd heard Kate had signed up for it.

"How was home ec?" Kate asked. "I think I'm taking that next. It's so nice you and Priti get to do it together!"

"It was . . . interesting," Zoey replied, still unsure of how she felt. She sat on the floor and put her legs out into a V, leaning forward slightly to each side to try and warm up her hamstrings. "Carter Perry is in the class, and he was joking around the whole time, of course. And there was this other boy, Sean Waschikowski. He fixed my machine for me when my needle jammed."

Kate's eyebrows shot up high. "He fixed *your* machine? Impossible."

Zoey laughed. "He did. He said he had the same machine at home. I wonder what kind of stuff he makes."

Kate looked thoughtful. "Sean, Sean. I *think* I know who you mean. He's tall and slim? He helped out with the costumes in the school's musical last year. Maybe he sews costumes."

"Hmm." Zoey was intrigued. She *did* like the idea of making new sewing friends. "I'll ask him."

Their tap teacher went to the front of the room and clapped her hands to signal the beginning of class.

"Oh, by the way," Kate whispered as they took their positions in line. "My physical therapist said my arm is pretty much all better! In about two more weeks I can start playing sports again!"

Zoey was so thrilled for her friend, she couldn't help throwing her arms around her in a hug. "That's so great, Kate! Why didn't you say something sooner?"

The warm-up music for their class came on, and Zoey had to release Kate so they could begin doing some shuffle, ball change steps.

"Would you believe I actually forgot?" Kate said with a giggle. "I've been having so much fun hanging out with you and Libby and Priti, and taking tap, and going to the movies, I'd almost forgotten how much I missed swimming and soccer!"

"Let's get together this weekend and celebrate," Zoey whispered. "I'm so happy for you!"

"Okay, I'll make a plan and tell everybody!"

"Eyes forward, ladies!" bellowed their teacher. "Mouths closed. Feet moving."

Zoey bit her lip to stop herself from smiling and focused on her steps. *Shuffle, ball change. Shuffle, ball change.*

On Wednesday, Lulu picked up Zoey after school and they drove to Zoey's favorite fabric store, A Stitch in Time. For Zoey, any trip to the fabric store was an exciting one, because there was nothing she liked better than to roam the aisles, touching different fabrics and imagining the outfits she could make with them. But today was a particularly important day, because Lulu had approved the final sketch for her wedding dress, and she and Zoey were going to select the fabrics for both the wedding gown and Zoey's junior bridesmaid's dress!

In the backseat Aunt Lulu's dog, Buttons, sat wagging her tail and emitting the occasional yelp of excitement. Buttons wasn't a very big dog, so she was occasionally allowed to join Lulu on errands, which she loved. Zoey reached her hand back to scratch Buttons under her chin, and she gave her a happy doggy smile.

At the store Lulu, Zoey, and Buttons (who was on a leash) were quickly greeted by Jan, the store's manager. She'd known Lulu for years, and had come to know Zoey very well also.

After giving both Zoey and Lulu a hug, Jan asked, "Well, ladies, what can I help you find today?"

Zoey looked at her aunt, who suddenly looked panicked. Apparently, Lulu had forgotten that Jan might be at the store and would certainly notice if Lulu was buying wedding gown fabric instead of pillowcase fabric, as she often did for her interior design jobs.

After a moment's indecision, Lulu shrugged, as if to say, *Oh well, what the heck*, and chuckled. "Jan, Zoey and I have a little secret to share. But we must keep it a secret, all right?"

Looking intrigued, Jan quickly agreed. "Of course! Tell me."

Lulu explained about her recent engagement,

the upcoming party/surprise wedding, and how Zoey would be making the wedding gown.

"Oh my word, you're kidding!" Jan cried. "That's just about the most wonderful, most *romantic* thing I've ever heard. And to have *Zoey* make the dress— it's too much. I might cry right here."

Zoey and Lulu laughed, because they knew Jan probably wasn't kidding. She was sentimental and just the type to get a tear in her eye while helping someone select their wedding dress fabric.

"If you only have a few weeks, we need to get down to business," Jan said. "Let me see the design, and we'll find you the perfect fabric."

Zoey produced the sketch, which Aunt Lulu had already seen and adored, and Jan oohed and ahhed over it. Zoey felt her arms and legs get warm and tingly, which is how she felt whenever someone complimented her work. She hoped the dress would look as good as the sketch when it was made!

"We need just the right fabric," Lulu said. "And Zoey seems to prefer the pearl-colored ones with a slight sheen."

"Pearlescent," said Jan. "Absolutely. And we'll need one with some good weight to it, to make your dress look its most elegant. I think that'll work with this structure, too. Let's go take a look."

The three of them, plus Buttons, headed over to the wedding gown fabrics. Zoey and Jan quickly zeroed in on one that would work, and Lulu agreed it was perfect. Next Jan gave them some suggestions for fabric that would work with Zoey's design for the junior bridesmaid's dress. Its combination of pink and red fabric would be easy for the maid of honor, Sybil, to coordinate with.

"I can't believe it was that easy!" Lulu said. "Now if only the sewing part was easy for Zoey . . ."

Zoey shrugged, smiling. "Don't worry about me. I'm ready for anything!"

"Is there something else I can help you find?" Jan asked.

Lulu nodded. "Some lace ribbon. We need it for trim and for some other decorative things."

They quickly found some ribbon in the notions department, and as Lulu was deciding how many spools of ribbon they should buy, Buttons jumped on her legs and barked excitedly at the ribbon, wagging her tail.

"Is she saying she likes it?" Jan asked with a laugh.

Zoey laughed too. Then she got an idea. "Oh my gosh! Lulu—we should have Buttons in the ceremony! She could be the ring bearer, even though she's a girl, and I could make her a little pillow with extra fabric from your dress and some of this ribbon. The ring can go in a little pocket, and she can walk it down the aisle. I saw it in a bridal magazine."

Lulu's face lit up. "Zoey, that's a *wonderful* idea! Buttons is a bit like my child, I suppose. It would be darling to have her as our ring bearer. Let's get some extra ribbon, and we'll do it!"

Jan rang up their purchases, and pleased with how much they'd accomplished, Lulu, Zoey, and Buttons headed back out to the car.

"How are all the other to-do list items for the wedding?" Zoey asked as they pulled out of the parking lot.

Aunt Lulu sighed. "Well, mostly okay. But John and I are having a lot of trouble finding a photographer. I've called everyone in town, and even nearby towns, and only found one person available!"

"One person is all you need, though, right?" asked Zoey.

"Yes, *but* . . . ," Lulu paused, shaking her head. "John and I had that person come by a few days ago to take some engagement photos for us, as a trial. And because I thought we'd use them on the invitations to the event. But the photographer just sent me the proofs this afternoon, and they are *terrible*."

"Terrible? Really?" Zoey was surprised. Her aunt was so beautiful, Zoey couldn't imagine a terrible picture of her.

Lulu shuddered and gripped the steering wheel tighter. "The photographer calls his style 'raw photojournalism,' which is apparently code for 'shows every flaw.' The photos make us look old and sickly! Dig in my purse for my phone and then look in my e-mail. You'll see it."

Zoey located her aunt's phone and opened up the e-mail application. She found the e-mail from the photographer and opened up the attachment with the proofs.

Lulu was right. Every picture was from an odd angle, with harsh lighting, and instead of looking warm and romantic and happy, John and Lulu looked like they were just getting over a bad case of the stomach flu.

"Um, they aren't the greatest," Zoey said. She wanted to be honest, but she didn't want to make Lulu feel any worse about them than she already did.

"I asked him if he could fix them for us; you know, touch them up, maybe Photoshop them—anything. But he refused. So we're at a standstill on the invites. I guess I'm going to end up calling people and inviting them over the phone!"

"Don't worry, Aunt Lulu," Zoey said soothingly. "You'll figure something out. You can always print up invites without photos, right?"

Lulu nodded. "We could, but I was so excited for the pictures. I love seeing couples on save-the-date cards and engagement invitations." She laughed. "Ah, well, it'll work out. I'm thrilled about the fabrics and Buttons's new job at the ceremony."

"Me too," Zoey agreed. "I'm going to start sewing tonight. With only two and a half weeks left, we don't have a moment to lose!"

"You've got that right. Whose idea was this surprise wedding, anyway?" Lulu said. "It's crazy."

Zoey just laughed.

----------- CHAPTER 5 -----------

Sew Zoey? *Chef* Zoey!

I knew that having electives at school would be fun, but I didn't know it would be *this* much fun! It's so nice to have a break from taking notes in classes all day (maybe not everyone does that, but I *have* to take notes to remember things) and go to my home ec elective! We started our aprons, and mine is going slowly, but it's kind of hard to concentrate with so much action in the sewing room. Every five minutes someone gets something stuck in a machine or sticks themselves with a needle. It's not exactly like working in my home "office" (a.k.a., the dining room)!

Anyway, today we're supposed to start cooking, which I can't wait to do, because right now my two specialties are pancakes, and brownies from a mix. And that's it! I'd like to learn to make at least a few other things. Like spaghetti.

For home ec class on Thursday, students had been told to meet in the cafeteria's kitchen. Their school didn't have a cooking classroom set up, since the electives structure was new, so the students would be using the large industrial kitchen instead. It was Zoey's first time back there, and she was amazed by how big it was and how enormous the walk-in fridges and freezers were. It was really neat!

"This is much cooler than I thought it would be," Priti whispered as the class huddled around Mrs. Holmes, who was preparing to demonstrate something in the prep space. "I love all these fancy pots and spatulas and things!"

Zoey nodded. "Me too. I can't wait to find out what we're making."

Mrs. Holmes clapped her hands and then said, "Let's begin. I think you're all going to like today's class, because we're going to be baking . . . molten chocolate cakes!"

A chorus of "yays" and "oh, yeahs" rang out from the group. What could be more fun than making chocolate cake?

Emily Gooding, a girl with long reddish-brown hair who stood close to Zoey and Priti, said pointedly, "I already know how to make those. My mother is a *chef*. She even makes her own pastries. Most chefs have to hire a pastry chef to do that."

Zoey resisted the urge to elbow Priti, because she was afraid Emily would notice. But she groaned inwardly. Since the home ec elective had begun, Emily had already mentioned about twelve times that her mother was a chef. Zoey thought it was very cool that Emily's mother was a chef, but the way she kept saying it made Zoey feel like Emily thought she was better than everyone else.

"Yes, we know, Miss Gooding," Mrs. Holmes said kindly. "In fact, I love your mother's restaurant. Would you like to come up and demonstrate for the class how to separate an egg white from the yolk?"

"Of course," said Emily, tilting up her chin and gliding to the counter to stand beside Mrs. Holmes.

Emily grasped an egg, cracked it confidently on the edge of a bowl, and watched as it splattered, bits of shell spraying into the bowl.

"Whoops," said Mrs. Holmes. "Why don't you try again?"

With slightly pink cheeks, Emily retrieved another egg from the carton on the counter and cracked it more carefully. As she was passing the yolk back and forth between the two halves of the shell, the yolk dropped into the bowl.

Emily looked up, stricken. Mrs. Holmes patted her shoulder. "That's quite all right, Emily. It happens! Would anyone else like to try?"

To Zoey's surprise, Priti's hand shot up in the air. Mrs. Holmes called on her, and Priti paused a moment to dig around in her backpack, retrieving a plastic water bottle. She quickly drank the last few sips of water and then carried the empty bottle to the prep counter and placed it beside the egg bowl.

"I know a really fun way to separate eggs," Priti said. "My mom showed me how to do this."

Priti's mom had a food blog called KarmaMama, and also used to run a catering business when Priti and her sisters were younger. Zoey knew Priti had a knack for baking, and she always seemed to have a suggestion for an ingredient that would make their cookies or brownies better, but Zoey didn't realize Priti probably knew a lot more than that.

"Show us," said Mrs. Holmes. "I'm intrigued!"

Priti delicately cracked an egg on the edge of a clean bowl and dumped the contents in, yolk and egg white together. Zoey heard Ivy and Bree snickering, and Bree clearly said, "Is she kidding with that? She didn't even *try* to separate the yolk."

"I think those goth clothes are making her dumber," Ivy said. "All that black is so depressing!"

Zoey coughed loudly to get Ivy's and Bree's attention, and then glared at them. She would *not* allow those girls to talk that way about her friend. Priti had been wearing a lot of all-black goth-type clothing lately, but fashion was about personal expression, and Zoey felt that everyone should be able to experiment with their clothing without having to listen to Ivy's opinions about it.

"So, I have the yolk and the egg white together in the bowl *on purpose,*" Priti said loudly, to show she'd heard Bree but couldn't care less. "And now for the trick!"

With her empty water bottle held upside down, Priti squeezed its body and then lowered it until the mouth of the bottle was on the yolk. Then she relaxed her hand, releasing her hold on the bottle, which created suction and immediately slurped the entire yolk right up into the bottle! Priti tilted the bowl toward the class, so they could see the perfectly separated egg white in the bowl, without a spot of yellow anywhere.

The students cheered. Priti repeated the trick several times, squeezing to release the yolk back into the bowl and then relaxing her hand to suck it back up into the bottle.

The class, except for Emily, Ivy, and Bree, clapped and whistled. Priti curtsied and then returned to her seat.

"Well done, Miss Holbrooke," said Mrs. Holmes. "It's a rare day in home ec when *I* learn something new. Thank you! Now, I've printed out lists of ingredients for you all, so please pair off and start collecting what you need. I'll set you up at stations, and we'll begin making our batter."

Priti returned to her spot beside Zoey, and Zoey reached over to give her a high five.

"Nice *work*, Priti," Zoey whispered. "You really showed the mean girls you're a cooking genius."

Priti beamed. "I love to cook. It's fun for me! How about you get us some bowls and spoons, and I'll gather the ingredients. We're partners, right?"

"You betcha," said Zoey.

The girls began making their cake batter side by side, talking as they worked. Zoey filled Priti in on the details of tap class and how Kate would soon be back to playing sports. And Priti told Zoey that she and Libby had gone to the movies the other night and seen the *worst* movie about a camping trip gone wrong, and she could still hardly sleep at night. Zoey tried to focus on her ingredients, but Priti's stories always made her laugh, and in the back of her mind, she was thinking about Lulu's wedding dress, which she had just started to cut out and baste. Before she knew it, Mrs. Holmes was standing in front of the girls, ready to taste their cakes.

Zoey's cake had just come out of the oven, and she hadn't even had a chance to taste it herself. But it looked amazing, and smelled wonderful, too. So she felt pretty confident it would be delicious.

Mrs. Holmes tried Priti's cake first, smiling as she held a bite in her mouth, and then nodded sharply. "Well done, Priti. I can tell you have a way with baking. And now you, Miss Webber."

Mrs. Holmes took a forkful of Zoey's beautiful cake and placed it in her mouth. Immediately, she made a tight, pinched face and reached for a paper towel to spit it out. "Oh *my*," she said.

"What?" asked Zoey, panicked. "I did everything Priti did! I measured so carefully. I think." Now that she thought about it, Zoey had tuned out a few times to worry about Lulu's dress, but still . . . She had checked off each ingredient on her list as she went along, just as Mrs. Holmes had told them to.

"Zoey, you made a very common error for a young chef. You mixed up the salt with the sugar! Better luck next time, my dear." Mrs. Holmes moved on to the pair beside Zoey.

Zoey picked up a fork and took a bite of her cake, then spit it right out. It was a disgusting, salty mess! She couldn't help giggling as she handed the fork to Priti to try. "It's reeeeeally awful. Try it!"

Priti shook her head. "No thanks, I'll eat mine!"

The girls watched as Mrs. Holmes walked around the large kitchen, tasting cake after cake. Emily did a good job, and so did Carter, surprisingly. Something had happened to Ivy's, and it hadn't baked properly.

"Oh, well, at least I can sew," said Zoey. "And you can bake. Together we're the perfect team." Then an idea occurred to her. "Hey, you should start a baking blog! You can call it *KarmaKid* or *KarmaCakes*."

"When would I have time?" Priti asked. "I'm so busy with school, and friends, and going back and forth between my mom's house and my dad's apartment. I don't think I could do one more thing."

Zoey nodded in agreement but thought about the many things she juggled—her schoolwork, her blog, her Etsy store, and now two dresses for Lulu's wedding. She was always doing a million things at once! *Of course*, Zoey thought, *I'm also the one with the salty cake!*

"Can I have a bite of yours?" Zoey asked Priti.

"Of course, Zo," Priti said. "Have as much as you want. I'm going to bake another one when I get home today, to practice. This was so much fun!"

"Do you think Ivy wants my cake?" Zoey asked jokingly. "I'm happy to share it with her."

Both girls laughed and then finished Priti's cake together before they had to clean up.

When Zoey got home from school, she saw a small package on the front porch. She picked it up, assuming it was for her father, and was delighted to find that it was addressed to her. The return address was New York, New York.

"A package from Daphne Shaw!" Zoey squealed. She hurriedly unlocked the front door and ran inside, dropping her backpack and plopping down on the couch to open her package. Daphne Shaw, otherwise known as Zoey's mentor and long-time commenter on Zoey's blog, was a famous designer. She always sent Zoey the most amazing, unique things, like little custom-made Sew Zoey labels for Zoey to sew into her clothes, and a special sticks-and-stones bracelet when Zoey was being cyberbullied. She was Zoey's fashion fairy god-mother and fashion idol.

Zoey hastily used her house key to slice through the packing tape and opened the box. Inside was a beautiful blue ring of fabric that looked like a large scrunchie. The fabric was toile, with a print with miniature images of couples sitting under trees, and had a tiny Daphne Shaw label on it. Beneath it was a note.

Dear Zoey,
Congratulations on being asked to design your first wedding dress! Who knows? You could be the next Vera Wang or

Monique Lhuillier. I made this garter especially for your aunt to wear on her big day. It's important not to forget the "something blue"!
Your friend, and
Fashionsista,
Daphne

Zoey was thrilled. She'd heard the saying "Something old, something new, something borrowed, something blue" for brides to wear on their wedding day, but with all the rushing around Aunt Lulu was doing, she wouldn't have time to think of it herself before the wedding. But Zoey would have this beautiful garter from Daphne Shaw to give to her, to make the day extra special. Zoey resolved to send a handwritten thank-you note to Daphne immediately.

"But first," she said to herself, "I've got about four hours of cutting and basting to do on Aunt Lulu's wedding gown. I wish I had some more of that molten chocolate cake to eat!"

CHAPTER 6

This Is *Not* the Dress!

Don't get excited, readers! This is not my aunt's dress. But being asked to design a wedding gown means spending tons of time reading wedding magazines and watching some of those wedding dress reality shows, so I *had* to sketch my own version of a princess gown. I could *never* make this—at least, I couldn't right now, because the beading and embellishments are so complicated. But I do think it's lovely! Particularly for a castle wedding, in a fairy tale, with a horse and carriage . . .

Anyway, it turns out I'm not a natural baker like my friend Priti. Apparently, you have to be very careful not to mix up the salt with sugar! I do love my home ec class, but I sometimes wish it was an advanced sewing course instead, so that I could learn a few more techniques for constructing gowns. If I'm going to make my aunt's dress, I want to be sure I get it right! Luckily, I have months to work on it. . . .

On Saturday morning Zoey woke up happy. She'd worked hard the evening before, sewing away on Lulu's dress, so that she could take the morning off and go to Libby's house. Libby had asked all the girls to come over and hang out, and Zoey couldn't wait to see her friends outside of school and *not* think about wedding chores for a few hours.

She took a shower and then belted a long

sweater over a pair of tights. She asked her dad if he could drop her off at Libby's. He had to head into work for a while, but her brother, Marcus, offered to take her.

On the way over, Zoey asked, "How are you doing practicing for Aunt Lulu's you-know-what?"

Marcus shrugged. "Okay, I guess. It's not that hard of a song to learn. I'm just nervous about playing it for her wed—for her you-know-what. It's not like just a concert or something, you know?"

Zoey nodded. "Oh, I know! I'm worried the dress I'm making her is going to fit badly, or she won't love it, or I won't finish in time and she'll have to wear some old thing in her closet. If it were anyone else . . ." Zoey let her voice trail off.

"But it's for Aunt Lulu," Marcus finished.

"Exactly," Zoey agreed.

Neither of them had to say what they were thinking: that for Lulu, who had been a stand-in for their mother since she'd passed away, they would do anything.

At Libby's house, Zoey thanked Marcus for the ride.

"I'm heading over to Allie's for a while," he said. "Call me when you need me to pick you up."

Allie Lovallo was Marcus's girlfriend and one of Zoey's best design pals. "Cool—tell Allie I said hi! See you later."

Zoey ran up to Libby's house and was pleased to see Priti and Kate just walking to the front door. The girls group hugged, as if they hadn't seen one another in forever, even though they'd all been at school the day before.

"Libby!" Zoey yelled, dropping her bag. "I miss you! We don't have enough classes together this semester. Tell me about your elective! I want to know everything."

Libby laughed. "Zoey, we eat lunch together *every day* at school. But come in, come in, let's go in the kitchen. My mom took Sophie and cleared out for the morning."

Sophie was Libby's little sister, who was in first grade. Zoey discovered Sophie's passion for interior design by mistake. Zoey's fabric scraps started going missing, and it turned out Sophie had used them to make rugs, pillows, and other decorations for her dollhouse, not realizing she was supposed to ask Zoey's permission before taking them. Now Zoey gave fabric scraps to Sophie on purpose. She handed Libby a bagful of them to give to her sister when she returned.

The girls all headed into the kitchen and took seats around the large island. Libby had made hot cocoa, and she poured some into mugs for everyone.

"Zoey and I learned how to make molten chocolate cakes in home ec the other day," Priti said. "We could make some to snack on, if you guys have semisweet baking chocolate. The rest of the ingredients are just flour, butter, eggs, and regular stuff."

Libby checked the pantry. "Got them!" she yelled. "My mom won't mind if we use the oven, as long as we remember to turn it off when we're done."

Priti quickly looked up the recipe on her phone, and placed it on the counter.

"I'm not so good at baking, you guys," Kate said. "But I'll help stir or whatever since I'm officially two-armed again!"

"Yay!" Zoey cheered. "Have you decided what

you're going to do about swimming yet?"

Kate had had to sit out from swim team for the whole semester so far and after being voted captain in the summer during preseason swim camp.

Kate nodded. "Yep—I already talked to my coach. I'm back on the team." She beamed. "I'm just not myself when I'm not on a team. I miss it too much!"

"Good for you, Kate," said Libby. "You love it, and you should do it! Even if we see you a little less."

The girls began gathering ingredients and bowls to make the cakes. Luckily, it wasn't a very complicated recipe, particularly with Priti supervising, and soon they had the cakes in the oven.

"So how's woodshop?" Priti asked Kate.

"Industrial *arts*," Kate corrected her.

"Industrial arts, then," Priti said with a grin.

"It's great," Kate replied. "I'm learning a lot. There are more girls in the class than I thought there would be, and it's really like an art class, except we're making things with plywood and jigsaws. I've started my first big project."

"What is it?" asked Libby. She set the timer for

the oven and came to sit beside Kate at the island.

"A snowboard!" Kate grabbed a piece of paper and a pencil and did a quick sketch of the board. "Since my arm is finally better, my mom said I could learn to snowboard this winter."

"That's awesome, Kate!" said Priti. "You'll be great at it. I can't believe you can make that in woodshop. I mean, *industrial arts*."

Kate nodded. "I probably can't *really* use the board on the slopes, but I can turn it into a neat shelf in my room for trophies. I just wanted to make something different, something that was *me*. Lorenzo's in my class, and he thought it was a good idea too."

Zoey and Libby exchanged a glance over Kate's head but didn't say anything about Lorenzo thinking *everything* Kate said or did was a good idea. They didn't want to embarrass their friend.

"So what are you doing in your computer science class?" Kate asked Libby, quickly changing the subject. For a second, Zoey wondered if maybe Kate *did* know what they were all thinking about Lorenzo, and didn't want to give them a chance to say it.

Libby slapped the counter. "Oh! That's what I wanted to remember. My class is great—I'm learning so much neat web design stuff. And the other day I was thinking maybe I could make something for your blog, Zoey."

"Like what?" Zoey asked.

"Um, like some sort of animated button that spins or bounces. It could advertise your Sew Zoey store, and people could click through to see your designs."

"You can do that?" Zoey was impressed.

"Absolutely! I can make a bunch of things now. And Gabe is in the class with me, and he loves to play with photo-editing software, so he's shown me a bunch of other tricks, too."

The timer dinged, indicating the cakes were ready to come out, and at the same time an idea dinged in Zoey's mind. Gabe! Zoey knew he was a talented photographer. Maybe he could help her aunt fix those engagement photos from the "raw photojournalistic" photographer.

Libby pulled out the four small cakes from the oven and placed them on top of potholders on the counter. She turned off the oven. The cakes looked and smelled amazing.

Zoey resolved to call her aunt as soon as she left Libby's. Right now, she and her friends had some cakes to eat!

Marcus picked Zoey up a few hours later, and they headed home. Back at her sewing machine, Zoey worked steadily on Lulu's dress for a few hours, until the doorbell rang. She hopped up to get it, and she was happy to see her aunt Lulu standing there.

"Aunt Lulu!" Zoey said. "What are you doing here? Are you coming over for dinner?"

Lulu shook her head. "Not this time, Zoey. I wanted to stop by because I have great news! I found another photographer to shoot the wedding! He's above our price range and can only be there for two hours, because he's booked later that evening to shoot another wedding nearby, but I'm desperate. His portfolio is excellent, and I think we'll at least have pictures that don't make John and I look like we have the plague."

Zoey was relieved. She knew having this big to-do item off the list made her aunt happy. And it reminded Zoey she had news to tell of her own.

"That's awesome, Aunt Lulu. And *I* have an idea for how to fix your engagement photos. . . ."

Lulu tilted her head. "Oh? Do tell!"

"Well, my friend Gabe is a really talented photographer, and he's taken a bunch of classes about how to use photo-editing software. Maybe you could e-mail him the files, and he could adjust the lighting or add a filter or something?"

Aunt Lulu chewed her lip a moment. "I don't know, Zoey," she said slowly. "I'm not sure I feel comfortable asking one of your friends to edit another photographer's work. I don't even have the high-res files, just the proofs."

"He's so great," Zoey persisted. "Look, I'll show you some of his pictures."

Zoey ran over to where she'd left her cell phone beside her sewing machine and found a photo Gabe had taken recently of her and Kate at their tap recital. She ran back over to her aunt and showed it to her.

Aunt Lulu studied it. "Well, that *is* very good. I'm impressed."

Zoey found several more and showed them to her aunt. Lulu seemed to consider it a moment and then sighed. "I think I'm just going to order invitations with no picture on them. I simply can't wait any longer, or we'll have no guests at this big event we're planning! But thank you, Zoey, I appreciate the suggestion."

Zoey shrugged. "No problem, Aunt Lulu. I just want you to have everything you want."

Mr. Webber and Marcus came upstairs then, and Mr. Webber gave Lulu a quick hug. "Marcus was playing something for me in the basement, but I thought I heard your voice, Lulu. How's it all going with the you-know-what? Is John going nuts? Are you going nuts?"

Lulu laughed, but it sounded slightly shrill. "No, no. Well, yes, a bit. But it's all coming together. Throwing a surprise wedding in three weeks sounded more romantic and easy-breezy than it's actually turning out to be, but in the end I know we'll love it."

"You will," said Zoey's dad. "We're all looking forward to it so much."

"I've been practicing your song," Marcus said. "I'll be ready."

"Jack," Lulu said to Mr. Webber, looking over Zoey's head. "Could the two of us talk for a moment? In private?" She smiled at Zoey and Marcus, as if nothing was out of the ordinary.

But something was out of the ordinary. Zoey could sense it. Her aunt wanted to talk to her dad alone? That never happened! She looked at Marcus for answers, but he looked as clueless as she was.

Zoey made a big fake sigh and said, "We know when we're not wanted. We'll go upstairs, and you can guys tell us when you're done talking."

"Nonsense," Mr. Webber said. "You've got sewing to do in the dining room, and Marcus needs to practice his guitar. Lulu can come up to my office for a second."

Zoey wondered if her dad knew what Lulu needed to talk to him about. You-know-what things? Finances? John? Even though Lulu was their mother's and not their father's sister, Lulu had been such a fixture in their house over the years that Zoey knew Lulu viewed Zoey's father almost as a real brother and not just a brother-in-law.

The adults went upstairs, and Marcus looked at Zoey. "That was weird. I'm going downstairs to practice. Tell me if you overhear anything."

Zoey agreed, and she got back to work on the gown, her mind unable to come up with a single thing her aunt couldn't say to Zoey's father in front of her and her brother. After about ten minutes, her father and aunt came downstairs, both of them smiling, and her aunt told her good-bye.

"I think I'll have the dress ready for your first fitting on Tuesday," Zoey said. She was still bursting with curiosity, but she knew she ought to respect her aunt's privacy. "I can bring it by if you want."

"Perfect, Zoey." Aunt Lulu grinned, seeming a bit more jolly than when she'd arrived. "See you then."

CHAPTER 7

Skorts and Skates!

One of my favorite things is looking at costumes worn by dancers, ice-skaters, and other sporty peeps. They have to be supercomfortable and practical to survive all those spins and twirls! I sketched my own fun and funky skating outfit, because I was supposed to go to the roller-skating rink today with my friends, but I've got a *ton* of sewing to do and I can't make it. Luckily, I saw the girls yesterday, and we caught up on everyone's news *and* baked delicious chocolatey treats *and* I didn't mix up any ingredients this time.

Hopefully, I can make this outfit soon and go skating next time. Sometimes a designer's work is never done. . . . (Pretending to sigh but actually too busy to have *time* to sigh!)

Zoey tried not to feel sorry for herself as she called Libby to cancel on roller skating. Libby was the one who always liked to plan fun things for everyone to do, and skating had been her idea as a perfect way to celebrate Kate's arm healing.

"Hello?" Libby answered cheerfully.

"Hi, Libs, it's me."

"Zoey! Are you almost ready? I bet you made something *fantastic* to wear. I'm wearing leggings and a short skirt and a sweater. I'm worried I'm going to fall a million times, and if I wear tights, I'll just rip them."

Zoey sighed. "Libby, I'm sorry—I can't go."

"*What?* Why?"

Zoey knew she had to be careful. She couldn't reveal the surprise wedding, but she didn't want to lie to her best friends, either. And, really, she didn't want to risk hurting their feelings. So she said, "I've started working on my aunt's wedding dress, and even though the wedding isn't for a while, I want to get it done as soon as possible, so there's time to fix it and add to it and make it perfect for her."

Libby was silent a moment. "Oh, um, okay. I thought Aunt Lulu hadn't even set a date, though? You need to work on it *today*?"

Zoey gritted her teeth. Was there any possible way to make it sound plausible? "Well, I've got Etsy orders, too, and they need to be done right away. And it's all just . . . so much." Then another idea hit her. "Aunt Lulu says she can't plan some things for the wedding, like accessories and bridesmaids' dresses, until she knows exactly how the wedding dress is going to look."

As Zoey said this, she nearly slapped herself on

the forehead. She'd totally forgotten she still had to sew her own junior bridesmaid's dress! She had the fabric and the design, but it was still going to be a lot of work!

"Okay, I get it." Libby sounded sympathetic. "You're really nice to do all that for your aunt, Zoey."

"It's no big deal," Zoey said. "But I *am* very sorry to miss going with you guys today."

"We'll miss you, too," Libby promised. "And I'll send you some pictures! Kate will probably be whizzing around backward on her skates while Priti and I cling to the wall and try not to get run over!"

Zoey laughed, as she could picture that scene perfectly. Kate did always manage to learn a new sport about ten times faster than anyone else. "Good luck," Zoey said. "Watch out for bumps!"

Zoey hung up and surveyed her worktable, mostly covered by her aunt's wedding gown. It was really starting to come together, and she knew if she worked hard all day, she'd probably have it ready for Lulu to try on in two days. Zoey turned on her sewing machine and then headed to the kitchen to make herself some hot chocolate. Just because she wasn't skating, it didn't mean she had to miss out on everything!

In home ec class on Monday, it was back to working on aprons. Zoey had really enjoyed their baking lesson in the cafeteria last week, even though her cake hadn't turned out especially well. But it was a fun break from being in a classroom, and she felt like she'd really learned something. The apron project was a challenge for most of the class, but Zoey couldn't help feeling a little resentful that with all the *real* sewing work she needed to be doing at home, she was spending time in class pinning together an apron.

Priti, however, had become very enthusiastic about sewing. She'd liked it from their first day, and she played and played with her sewing machine, trying to understand how its features worked, and looked at her basic apron pattern from different angles to see what could be done to improve her design.

"I just love this project," Priti said as she was basting together her fabric.

Zoey, whose apron was half-sewn already, had been debating adding pockets to the front when she'd gotten an idea about how to fix the underskirt of her aunt's wedding gown and had stopped to grab a piece of paper to sketch it and write it down before she forgot the idea.

"Zoey?" Priti said. "Are you listening?"

Zoey snapped to attention and looked over at Priti. "Yeah, sorry. What?"

Priti squinted. "Are you okay, Zoey? You look a little . . . stressed out." Priti peered over Zoey's fabric and saw the tiny sketch Zoey had just made of the gown. "Libby said you've been working really hard on your aunt's dress."

Zoey nodded. That was true, and it didn't give away anything secret.

"You know," Priti said, "I'm learning to sew now, so if you want some help, I'd be really happy to do it. I know I'm *nowhere near* as good as you are sewing-wise, or anything, but, I mean, if you just have something simple you need done, I could do it."

Zoey was grateful to her friend, but she didn't

know how she could accept Priti's offer without revealing the secret. If Priti came over to her house and saw all the wedding dress madness going on, she'd probably guess the wedding was imminent.

"Thanks, Priti," Zoey said as Mrs. Holmes passed by, giving Zoey a slight frown when she saw that Zoey wasn't working. "I'll let you know! I guess I'd better work on my apron right now, huh?"

Priti looked over at Mrs. Holmes. "Probably. I don't think she liked your cake very much. . . ."

The two girls giggled, and Zoey vowed to concentrate harder for the rest of the class. But even with her best effort, she couldn't stop thinking about her junior bridesmaid's dress and when on Earth she was going to find time to get it done.

Later that afternoon, Zoey realized that if she was going to finish her homework *and* have the wedding gown ready for Lulu to try on after school the next day, she'd have to skip tap class. Tap was a standing date with Kate, her oldest friend in the world, whom Zoey knew she soon wouldn't be seeing much of, since Kate was officially back on the swim team. But Zoey had no choice. The wedding was now in just about a week and a half. She *had* to get an initial fitting done right away or there wouldn't be time to get all the details right.

Kate answered the phone after the first ring. "Hi, Zo! I'm ready for class. My mom offered to drive both ways if we need her to. She says she can run to the grocery store while we're in class."

Kate's excitement made it even harder for Zoey to say what she had to say. "That's so nice of your mom, but I don't think I can go tonight. . . ."

"Why?" Kate sounded worried. "Are you sick? Did something happen?"

Zoey was really beginning to dislike these conversations with her friends, where she had to let them down *and* not be truthful about it. If she could just tell them the truth, they'd understand perfectly. They all knew Lulu and what an honor it was for Zoey to be making her gown.

"I'm not sick," Zoey said, wanting to stick to the truth as much as possible. "But I've got a *ton* of homework, and I'm working on some . . . stuff . . . for Lulu, to help her plan her wedding."

Kate sniffed. "But, you missed roller-skating yesterday. I thought you'd gotten all that 'stuff' done?"

"I know, Kate, and I'm really sorry." Zoey thought hard. What could she possibly say to make Kate understand and not sound as if her feelings were hurt? "Okay, listen. I haven't mentioned this to anyone, but Lulu asked me to make her an . . . *engagement* dress to wear to her engagement party next weekend, and it's such short notice that I'm working on it night and day."

"Wow! Really? How fun!" Immediately, Kate's tone changed. Zoey wished she'd thought of the "engagement dress excuse" before. "What's it look like?"

"Uhhh," Zoey said, stalling. "I'm not supposed to say. Because she wants it to be a surprise. For John."

"Well, I'm not going to *tell* him or anything. But, okay, I understand." Kate sounded like her normal, happy self again. "I'm going to go get ready for class. You get to work! If we learn any new steps tonight, I'll show them to you at school this week, okay?"

"Great," said Zoey, feeling hugely relieved. "Thanks for understanding."

"Sure!" said Kate. "I'll miss you, but that's life when you're best friends with a famous designer."

"*Famous* might be pushing it," Zoey protested.

"You've had a design on the cover of *Celebrity* magazine, a T-shirt you made worn by tween heart-throb Cody Calloway, and you've been a judge on *Fashion Runway*. It's time to stop being modest, Zoey."

"Okay, you're right. I guess I'm *kinda* awesome." Zoey giggled.

"Ha-ha, Zoey. Even when you're just pretending to be full of yourself, no one would believe it. Anyway, get to work. TTYS."

After school on Tuesday, Marcus kindly offered to drive Zoey and the wedding gown over to Lulu's for the fitting. Zoey wrapped it carefully in tissue and then zipped it into a garment bag. She was so paranoid about something happening to the dress that she'd been wrapping it up in fabric each night when she was finished working on it, just in case some dust from her house landed on it.

When they got to Lulu's, Marcus volunteered to take Buttons for a long walk, so Zoey and Lulu could do the fitting. They headed up to Lulu's bedroom, where she had a closet with a full-length mirror. When Zoey unzipped the garment bag, unpacked the tissue, and revealed the dress, Lulu gasped.

"Oh, Zoey, it's gorgeous already! Just look at it!" She paused, staring at the dress with wonder and emotion. She looked like she might even tear up, and the dress was only half-completed! "We certainly chose the right fabric. This pearlescent sheen is lovely."

"Phew—I'm so glad you like it!" Zoey exclaimed. "You have no idea how nervous I am working on it. I never use white fabric, and definitely not really *expensive* white fabric, so I've been wearing gloves half the time, so I don't get any finger oil or anything on it."

"That's clever, Zoey!" Aunt Lulu said. She stepped out of her suit and began, with Zoey's help, to pull on the dress. Some of the underskirt was still held together with pins, so they had to be very careful not to rip them out, prick Lulu, or damage any of the basting threads. "Where'd you get that idea?"

"From Jan," Zoey said. "She mentioned it to me at the store."

With the dress on, standing in front of the mirror, Lulu looked at herself. Slowly, she smiled and looked over at Zoey. "This is going to be *perfect*, Zoey. It's exactly what I want! And that's so important to me, particularly since we've had to compromise a bit on the invitations, and the photographer, you know."

Zoey nodded. She was thrilled her aunt looked so happy *and* that the dress seemed to fit well so far. She didn't see any major problems—just some tweaks here and there. Zoey got more pins and began to check over the seams in the underskirt, which needed to be loose enough to allow her aunt to dance, but strong enough to support the shape of the overskirt.

"How's your dress coming along?" Lulu said. "I hate to even ask! Have I overloaded you?"

Zoey shook her head. "No! I'm fine. My dress is . . . well, not done. I've cut out the pieces, but I haven't done anything to it yet. I'll get to it."

"If it's too much, Zoey, just tell me, and I'll run out and buy you a dress. I want you to have fun at this surprise wedding, too, you know!"

Zoey smiled. "I will. Don't worry! I'm so glad this dress is working out and we don't see any problems. I'm sure I'll be able to get everything done, and it'll be fine."

Lulu paraded around in the mirror admiring herself in the dress for another ten minutes or so, until they heard Marcus downstairs returning with Buttons. Then Zoey had to help Lulu take off the dress and then repack it carefully in the bag. Maybe it was costing her some time with her friends, and a little bit of stress, but the honor of making her aunt's wedding gown, and of making her so happy, was worth it to Zoey.

In home ec class the next day, Zoey and Priti were side by side, working on their aprons, and Zoey was worrying. Even though she'd told her aunt that everything was fine and that she'd be able to get both dresses completed before the event the following weekend, in her heart, she just didn't know when she'd have time to sew her junior bridesmaid's dress. For a second she thought about texting her aunt and taking her up on the offer to buy a store-bought dress, but then Zoey realized there was no way she'd love any dress as much as the one she'd designed.

"Zoey, look at you!" Priti exclaimed. "Your forehead is all wrinkled and your mouth is puckered like you just ate a lemon. What's *wrong*?"

Zoey sighed heavily. She couldn't stop fretting. Especially while sewing on her apron, which seemed rather silly compared to the wedding dress she was making at home.

"You might as well tell me," Priti said, sounding both friendly and threatening at the same time. "I'll get it out of you somehow!"

Zoey couldn't help smiling a little bit. Priti was tenacious. Zoey *had* to tell her something. She decided to adapt the story she'd told Kate, since it was the most truthful thing she was allowed to say. She really hated lying to her friends.

"Get what out of her?" asked Sean, butting into

their conversation. "What are you hiding, Zoey Webber?"

Sean was standing at the machine to the right of Zoey, helping another student to get it working again. He finally got the needle humming, and he moved a step closer, so he could be in front of Zoey and Priti.

"Sorry I was eavesdropping, but I *love* secrets." Sean smiled and shrugged, as if he couldn't help himself.

Zoey knew she had to say something, because Sean didn't seem like the type to give up easily. "Well, it's not a secret, exactly. But I designed a junior bridesmaid's dress for myself, to wear to my aunt's wedding, and now I've decided to wear it to her engagement party instead, and I have less than ten days to make it!"

"Is it the design you posted on your blog?" Sean asked. "It has, like, one shoulder, with what looked like a bubble skirt hem?"

Zoey nodded, both flattered and surprised that Sean knew exactly which design she'd been talking about.

"But that dress is beautiful, Zoey!" Priti said. "It would be such a shame if it didn't work out."

"I know," Zoey agreed. "But unless I can wear it held together with safety pins, I just don't know how I can make it and the dress my aunt is wearing to the engagement party. And she's the bride-to-be, so hers is the most important out of the two dresses to make!"

Sean seemed to think a moment. Nervously, he fiddled with the hand wheel on Zoey's machine. "If you want, I could help you," he said shyly. "I mean, I've done a lot of sewing. Not as much as you, but I made all the costumes for the school musical last year. And I'd follow your design exactly."

"Really? You would do that?" Zoey was flabbergasted. It was an incredibly nice offer, and from someone she hardly even knew! She immediately felt an overwhelming sense of guilt that she'd been slightly envious of Sean ever since that first day of home ec. Sean managed to win praise from the class every day by keeping all the machines running smoothly, and no one really even mentioned Zoey being in the class anymore. She probably could have been a little friendlier to him during the beginning of the apron competition.

But now it seemed she *did* have a chance to really become friends.

"I would *love* that, Sean," Zoey said. "But do you have time? Honestly? Could you really do it?"

Sean grinned again. "Of *course.* I'd be happy to help produce a Sew Zoey original. How about I come by your house after school today to get the materials?"

Zoey nodded quickly, feeling like a huge weight had been lifted off her shoulders. Even though she'd never thought about having someone else sew together her dress, she already had the fabric cut out, and Sean really did seem to be the perfect solution to her problem. She knew he could do a great job.

"Wow, I really owe you one!" Zoey said. "If you ever need help with *anything*, just ask."

"I'll remember that," he said, grinning. "Now get back to work on your apron. Mrs. Holmes is coming, and you look like you haven't even threaded your machine yet. . . ."

········· CHAPTER 8 ·········

A Friend to the Rescue!

I've gotten used to all my awesome girlfriends helping me out from time to time with projects and ideas and homework. And I try to do the same for them in return! But for the first time I've made friends with a *boy*, who is pretty awesome with a sewing machine, and he offered to help me finish the dress I'm wearing to my aunt's engagement party next week. I'm not going to write his name here, because I get the feeling he's still a little shy about being known as "the guy who sews" (even though it's *awesome*), but he knows who he is. I sketched this outfit for him, because it seems like his style and something he could really rock at school.

Not only have I been a busy bee helping my aunt get ready for her engagement party, but my grandparents are coming for the party, too—all the way from Arizona! I haven't seen them since last Christmas, so I'm very, very excited. Only one more week to wait! ☺

On the Sunday before the wedding, Aunt Lulu came over to Zoey's house for another fitting.

"It feels pretty good, Zoey. How does it look?" Aunt Lulu asked. She stood in front of the mirror, turning left and right, admiring herself.

"It lookth almoth thone! I can'th believe how few alterationth it needth!" Zoey was holding a few straight pins in her mouth, which made it hard to talk.

"Oh good, I'm so glad." Aunt Lulu exhaled deeply, and she seemed to relax. Unfortunately, that shifted some of the pins. "Things are set with the caterers, and the house is being cleaned at the end of the week, and I *think* I've got an idea for a little wedding gift for John, just something small. . . ."

Lulu chattered on while Zoey knelt down to checked the seams in the skirt of the dress. She'd basted them together already, and now she had to mark with pins the ones that needed to be sewn up on the machine.

"How's *your* dress coming?" Lulu asked.

"Great!" Zoey replied. "At least, I think it is. My friend Sean ended up doing the sewing work for me, and he said he's going to bring it by later today for me to try on."

"That's great news!" Aunt Lulu beamed. "I've been worried you were working too hard."

"Not at all," she assured her. "And remember, I'm getting some awesome experience! I've designed and made a wedding gown. I never, ever thought I could do that!"

Zoey stood up, and Lulu very carefully, since her bodice was still pinned, pulled Zoey close for a squeeze.

"I knew you could do it," Lulu said. "And I can't *wait* to tell all the guests that my very own, very talented niece made this gorgeous dress!"

"Well, it's still not totally done, so you'd better get out of it so I can finish!" Zoey joked. Today was her last full day to work on it, since she had school all week. Plus, her grandparents were coming to town on Thursday. Zoey *had* to get the dress completed.

After Lulu left, and Zoey had just gotten back to work, the doorbell rang again. Marcus and her father had offered to help John today by running errands for the you-know-what, so Zoey had to answer the door. She hurriedly threw a large white bedsheet over the worktable, to cover Lulu's dress. She didn't know who was at the door and didn't want to take a chance of anyone seeing it.

She was pleased to see Sean standing there, with her finished dress, all pressed and ready to wear.

"How on Earth did you do that so fast?" Zoey

asked, amazed. She looked the dress over from top to bottom, expecting to see something he'd missed. But there was nothing. It looked perfect. "I can't believe it!"

"Well, it was *your* design, and you'd cut it out, so I didn't have to agonize over every design decision as I made it, like you probably would have," Sean said. "I just sewed it together! Do you want to try it on?"

Zoey nodded, and she ran upstairs to change. Luckily, Zoey had made herself so many outfits that she knew exactly what size she was and had cut the fabric accordingly, so the dress fit like a glove. It looked terrific.

She ran downstairs to show Sean. She stopped at the bottom of the steps and did a twirl.

Sean applauded. "It's great!" he said. "You'll be the best bridesmaid there."

Cheeks flaming, Zoey stopped her twirling. "What do you mean?" she asked. Anxiously, she tried to remember their conversation. Had she accidentally revealed the secret?

Sean looked confused by her obvious panic.

"Didn't you say you were a junior bridesmaid? You'll be the best one at the engagement party."

Zoey realized he meant that she'd be the best *of* the junior bridesmaids there (although she was the only one), not that she'd actually be performing her junior bridesmaid's duties quite yet. She breathed a sigh of relief, both at having not been caught and also because this hideous secret keeping was nearly over. Only a few more days, and she could go back to her regular, *honest* life!

"I can't thank you enough, Sean," Zoey said. "You *saved* me, you really did. I'm sorry I haven't . . . I mean, I'm sorry we haven't had a chance to get to know each other very well at school. Maybe we could hang out sometime."

Sean shrugged casually. "No worries. It was a great project for me. I love making clothes, but it's not something that's very popular for guys at Mapleton Prep to do, you know?"

Zoey nodded. "Yeah. I do know."

Sean looked at her slyly. "Remember how you said you'd owe me?" He wiggled his eyebrows up and down, as if mimicking a villain from a cartoon.

"Yeeeees?" Zoey asked seminervously.

Sean coughed before he said, "Would you want to help me start a fashion club at school? I've been wanting to do it for a while, but until we had this home ec elective, I didn't think there would be enough kids who knew how to sew. But if you did it with me . . . I mean, I think it would be really cool."

"I love that idea!" Zoey exclaimed. Her brain immediately started to explore the possibilities. "Let's do it!"

"Shake on it?" Sean asked, holding out his hand.

Zoey shook it firmly, and the deal was struck. Zoey couldn't believe her good luck. She'd found a cool new design friend, had a finished junior brides-maid's dress, *and* they had a plan to create a new club at school.

"Well, I've got to get going," Sean said. "But I'll see you at school tomorrow, okay?"

"I can't thank you enough, Sean, really!" said Zoey.

Zoey walked Sean to the door and waved as he headed off toward his house. She glanced at the clock and realized she really needed to hurry and get back to work. But first, she had to put her own clothes back on.

Upstairs, just as she was getting back into her tunic and leggings, the doorbell rang again.

"Good grief, who is *that*?" Zoey wondered.

Then she remembered she'd asked Priti to come by and help her pin the junior bridesmaid's dress on herself, so she could make adjustments, because she didn't know Sean would do such an unbeliev- able job. Usually, she pinned things on herself, but it was awkward to do, and she wanted this dress to look flawless for her aunt's wedding.

Zoey hurried back down the stairs, carrying the junior bridesmaid's dress on a hanger. She checked to see that the bridal gown was still covered, and satisfied the secret was safe, she opened the door.

"Hi, Priti!" Zoey said breezily, as if nothing were ever amiss.

"Is *that* the dress?" Priti said. "WOW—it's beau- tiful! And Sean sewed that?"

Priti came inside and followed Zoey into the living room. She inspected the beautiful dress from top to bottom. "I'm really impressed," Priti said. "He did a great job. How's it fit?"

Zoey's face broke into a smile. "You won't believe this, but it's perfect! I'd cut it out very carefully, and gave him my measurements, but even so, I expected it to be a little loose or tight or whatever. But it's not! It's totally ready to go. I don't even need you for alterations help!"

"That's amazing," said Priti. She paused and bit her lip, her eyes fixed on the dress. "Um, I know you said you designed this to wear for the wedding . . ."

Immediately, Zoey became nervous once again. Priti looked like she was holding back something important. "What is it, Priti?"

"It's just . . . well . . ." Priti sighed. "To be honest, I'm not sure you should wear it to the engagement party. It's *so* special, and perfect for a bridesmaid. It's the nicest bridesmaid's dress I've ever seen! I just think you might want to save it for the wedding instead, and wear a regular dress to the engagement party."

Priti looked down, as if worried she would hurt Zoey's feelings. But instead, quite by accident, she'd said the absolute perfect thing.

"Really? You think so?" Zoey beamed. She loved the dress too, and she thought it was perfect for the wedding, but it was nice to hear it from someone else. "Okay, then I think maybe I *do* want to wear it for the wedding." Zoey tried not to laugh as she said this.

Relieved, Priti flopped down onto the sofa. "Can I stay for a minute, or do you need to work?" She leaned toward the coffee table, and picked up the roll of lace ribbon that Buttons had picked out at A Stitch in Time. "I just don't feel like going home."

"Sure," Zoey said automatically, although she really did need to get back to work. But something in Priti's tone kept her from saying that.

Before Zoey could ask what was going on, Priti held up the ribbon. "What's this?" she asked. "It's very pretty."

With a gasp, Zoey realized she'd completely forgotten the third project she'd promised for Lulu's wedding: the ring bearer pillow for Buttons to wear! How could she have forgotten?

"Th-that's, uh, um . . . ," Zoey stammered. "That's to make a ring bearer pillow for Aunt Lulu's dog,

Buttons. Isn't that neat? She's going to walk the ring down the aisle."

Priti's eyes went wide, and she laughed. "You're kidding! I love that! What a fun idea."

"But, Priti, I can't believe it, but I—I forgot to make it!" Suddenly, a thought occurred to Zoey. Priti was at her house, with time to spare, and was learning to sew in home ec. Zoey needed help getting the pillow done. What if she asked Priti to do it while she supervised? She would have to tell Priti she's been working on the wedding dress in secret, and still not mention anything about the surprise wedding.

She decided to go for it. "Priti, would you help me out and make the ring bearer pillow? I've got my extra sewing machine here, and I could show you how Lulu wants it to look. It's a great project for a beginner, and we can chat and catch up while I work on my aunt's gown."

Priti looked stunned. "You'd let me help? Oh, I'd love to, I'd really love to!" She was quiet a moment, then asked, "Do you really have your aunt's wedding gown started already? Can I see it?"

Zoey nodded, and led Priti to her worktable in the dining room. She pulled back the bedsheet to reveal the beautiful pearlescent gown.

"Zoey, you've been working on *this*?" Priti shook her head in disbelief. "I can't believe it. How can you stand home ec class?"

Zoey burst out laughing. "I love home ec. I get to hang out with you! And we made those awesome cakes with the gooey chocolate inside."

Priti picked up a scrap of the wedding gown's fabric, smoothing it between her fingertips. Zoey pointed. "That's what we'll use to make the little pillow. Let me go get my other machine, and we'll get to work!"

Zoey retrieved the fancy Speedman machine she'd received as a gift when her mom's machine broke. She cleared a space for it on the dining room table. The she made a quick sketch of the pillow, with measurements for Priti to use as a pattern, and found some batting to use for the inside.

"So, there will be a little pocket *here* for the ring, and that's about it," Zoey said, explaining the basic design. "I'm so glad you're helping me with it!

My grandparents are coming later this week, and I know they'd love to see it. Plus, I really don't have time!"

The two girls sat down alongside each other to work, and Zoey was happy to have her friend there with her. Priti always made everything more fun.

Then Zoey remembered the comment Priti had made earlier. "Hey, how come you said you didn't want to go home? Is something going on?"

Priti was measuring the scrap of gown fabric carefully and holding it up to check with Zoey before she cut it.

"Um, well, no," Priti said. "There's nothing *new* going on. I just can't get used to going back and forth every few days between my mom's house and my dad's apartment. And my sisters are never ever at either place, because they're in high school, and they're always gone all the time, so it's just *me* sitting there with whichever parent. So it's kind of lame."

Priti was still wearing the dark, bleak goth clothing she'd begun wearing when her parents split up over the summer. Zoey had hoped that as school got underway, Priti'd go back to her previous wardrobe of fun, bright colors, and accessories with sparkle. But she hadn't.

"Is there anything I can do, Priti?" Zoey asked. "You know you can always hang out here. And Sean and I might start a fashion club! You could join that. It'll probably be after school."

"Great idea!" Priti said. "I definitely will. And thanks, but I'm okay. My new 'parental situation'— that's my what sisters call it—will just take time to get used to, I guess."

The girls worked in silence for several minutes. Priti seemed happy to be there, and she was doing a great job with the pillow. Zoey couldn't help feeling like she'd gotten very lucky to have help from both her and Sean.

As Zoey was finishing up the hem on the wedding gown, she noticed Priti looking at it oddly.

"What?" Zoey asked. She immediately scanned the dress for flaws. "Do you see a smudge?"

Priti shook her head. "Nooooo," she said. "I just think it's odd that you're so far along on the wedding dress when there's *still* no date for the wedding. And this pillow . . ."

She let her voice trail off. Zoey could see Priti mentally adding up the wedding gown, the ring bearer pillow, and the junior bridesmaid's dress. Priti had probably guessed what was really going on, but was kind enough not to say it out loud. Zoey knew Priti could keep a secret, and she longed to tell her, but Zoey had promised her aunt, and she meant to keep that promise.

"Aunt Lulu just wants to show everything to my grandparents ahead of time," Zoey said, rather limply. "They're coming this week, you know."

Priti nodded. "Sure, that makes sense."

The girls continued working, but Zoey began to feel guilty. She hadn't been able to keep the secret after all. She'd tried her best, but, somehow, it seemed it might have slipped through the seams.

CHAPTER 9

Smaller Is Better (For Now!)

I'm thinking of taking a break from big, elaborate sewing projects for a while. . . . I'm wiped out! I've been working on a lot of complicated dresses recently, and even though they're very satisfying to complete, they are very tiring to work on! ☺ I know that if I take a little break and make some new accessories for my Sew Zoey store, I'll be energized and ready to get back to dresses again. Everyone needs accessories, and people seem to like buying them online, because they're one size fits all!

I *can't* talk about all the big things happening in the next few days, but I *can* say that they're all I can think about! My aunt's dress for her engagement party is nearly done, and my dress is completely done, but I'm helping with some other details as well. I'm not sure I've ever felt this busy and frantic. I feel like I'm bursting at the seams. I'm just so excited and nervous and exhausted, all at the same time.

On Tuesday, Zoey asked Lulu to come over after school to try on the wedding dress one final time. Zoey was pretty sure it was finished and ready, but she wanted to leave herself enough time to make any final *final* changes. She paced nervously by the front door waiting for her aunt to arrive.

Aunt Lulu was ten minutes late, and she showed up looked flushed and flustered. "I'm sorry, Zoey," she said. "Last-minute wedding phone calls. The company that was delivering the tables and chairs thought the party was *next* Saturday! Thank goodness I called to confirm."

Zoey ushered Lulu upstairs, and they went into Zoey's bedroom. The dress hung on Marie Antoinette, Zoey's dress form, steamed and pressed and looking gorgeous.

Lulu eyes teared up again when she saw the gown, and Zoey couldn't help feeling glad for all the many, many hours she'd put in to make the dress as perfect as she could. Lulu slipped out of her pants and blouse, and Zoey helped her step into the gown. Lulu pulled a beautiful pair of pearl-colored satin sling-back heels from her purse and put them on.

"I bought these because the heel's height was exactly what you and I had planned on," Lulu said. And she was right. The hem of the dress just kissed the floor when the shoes were on.

As Zoey zipped up the back of the dress, she examined the bodice for any puckers or wrinkles that needed her attention. Lulu admired herself in the mirror, the sparkle in her eyes telling Zoey all she needed to know about how Lulu felt about the dress.

To Zoey's delight, and relief, the dress appeared to be done. It fit well, it moved well, and it was even the right length. Zoey couldn't believe it. She'd finished her first wedding gown! And she couldn't help thinking that maybe she had a knack for them. Could she really be a future Monique Lhuillier or Vera Wang?

Lulu walked around the room several times in her new shoes and dress, beaming and looking every inch the beautiful bride. Zoey was glad Lulu didn't seem to want to take off the dress. That was a good sign.

"I think I'll even be able to dance in it!" Lulu exclaimed.

Then she paused at Zoey's closet door, where Zoey's junior bridesmaid's dress hung in a plastic dry-cleaner's bag, finished and ready for Saturday. "Oh, Zoey!" Lulu said. "It's even more beautiful than I thought it would be! And it'll look great with Sybil's maid of honor dress, although I know she'll be jealous when she sees how adorable yours is."

Zoey grinned. She couldn't wait to wear her dress. "The ring pillow is ready too," Zoey said, picking it up from her desk and showing it to Lulu.

Lulu ran her fingertips over the lace ribbon and dress fabric on the pillow. "It's just lovely," she said softly. "I can't imagine how a busy student like you managed to get this all done."

"Well, I had a little help from my friends," Zoey admitted. "Actually, a *lot*. Or I never would have been able to do it all! My friend Sean sewed the junior bridesmaid's dress together, and Priti made the pillow." She cleared her throat. "The hardest thing, really, has been keeping the secret from everyone. I've told so many ridiculous stories about why I've been so busy, I'm sure everyone thinks I've lost it!"

Lulu laughed. "Me too! No one can believe I haven't set the date for the wedding yet, since they all know John and I are thinking of starting a family sometime soon. I've said all kinds of absurd things. I feel like I might burst from keeping it all in!"

"Starting a family? Like, having kids? That

would be so amazing to have a baby cousin!" Zoey squealed. "You know, I feel like I could burst too. But it's almost Saturday. We can do it."

Lulu reached for Zoey's hand. "We can do it," she repeated. "And I have a little something special to give to you to top off your beautiful dress for the big day." Lulu walked over to her purse, pulled out a large velvet sachet, and handed it to Zoey.

"Oh!" Zoey exclaimed when she loosened the drawstring and peeked inside. She pulled out a beautiful headband topped with a row of pearls.

"Here, let me help you," Aunt Lulu said. She brushed Zoey's hair back with her fingers and gently placed the headband on Zoey's head.

"It's perfect, Aunt Lulu! Thank you!" Zoey said.

"No, thank *you*!" Aunt Lulu gave Zoey a squeeze. "I couldn't have pulled this wedding off without you, sweetie."

At last, it was the night before the wedding.

Zoey's dad had planned a very informal "rehearsal dinner" at their house for John, Lulu, and Lulu's parents, who were in on the wedding surprise. Zoey was thrilled to have her grandparents come over, since they were staying at Lulu's house and Zoey had been at school during the day and hadn't been able to hang out with them. She'd gone over the night before to help Lulu and her grandmother tie up favors for the guests, and she'd had the chance to tell her grandparents all about school and her friends and her tap class. But it still wasn't enough time.

When the doorbell rang, Zoey raced to answer it first, but Marcus beat her to it. He hugged his grandparents, Bill and Dorothy Price, and then Zoey did the same. Zoey didn't remember her mother very well, and though she knew Lulu was a lot like her, whenever Zoey saw her grandmother Dorothy, she felt like she was getting a glimpse of her mother.

Mr. Webber offered everyone a drink, and the family sat down in the living room to chat. Zoey had put out cheese and crackers and some dip, which mostly Marcus ate. The doorbell rang again, and this time Mr. Webber went to answer it. Zoey knew it would be her aunt and John arriving, so she was surprised when the first thing she heard was a muffled sob and some sniffling when the door opened.

Lulu and John walked into the living room, Lulu clutching John with one hand and holding a tissue to her eyes with the other. Zoey wasn't used to seeing her aunt cry, so her alarm bells went off immediately.

Grandma Dorothy immediately stood up and went over to her daughter. "What is it, dear? What's happened? Nothing serious, I hope?"

John shook his head slightly, and Zoey felt momentary relief. At least no one seemed to be ill or anything.

Lulu blew her nose, and said, "I was having trouble getting hold of the photographer this week to confirm. I kept calling and calling. Finally, he called me back as we were driving over here, and he said that he'd made a mistake. He doesn't have two hours for us—he's actually already *booked for the exact same time.* He can't shoot our wedding."

Lulu took a deep breath to calm herself, and Grandma Dorothy put her arm around her.

"He's completely double-booked? How on Earth did that happen?" Mr. Webber said.

Lulu shook her head in disbelief. "He has some new scheduling system, and it didn't sync up correctly with the old system. So he thought he had two hours to shoot our wedding, but he doesn't. And he booked the other event first, so he has to honor their contract. So now it's the day before our wedding, and we don't have a photographer."

"It could be worse," Marcus chimed in. "You could not have a bride or groom."

"Not funny, Marcus," Mr. Webber snapped, but Aunt Lulu managed a small smile.

"Actually, Marcus is right," she said. "This is not the end of the world. It's just . . . not great."

Grandma Dorothy led Lulu to a chair and then went to the kitchen to get her a drink. She brought back a glass of water and handed it to her. "We'll solve this, dear, okay? We'll call some other photographers."

John said, "Well, we tried everyone else already. Saturdays are their busiest days, so they're all booked too."

"I can't believe there isn't *anyone* available for tomorrow," Mr. Webber said. "I'll take the pictures myself, Lulu, if you'd like."

Marcus laughed. "You take *terrible* pictures, Dad! You always cut off our heads."

Zoey wanted to defend her father, but it was true. "You do take bad pictures, Dad," she said. "But we love you, anyway."

"Well, thanks," said Mr. Webber. "Sort of."

Then Zoey had an idea, and she thought her aunt might be desperate enough to go for it.

"Aunt Lulu," she began, "remember my friend Gabe I told you about? The one who's taken all the photography classes? We could ask *him* to photograph the wedding, and maybe we could also buy a bunch of disposable cameras and put them on tables, to encourage the guests to take photos, too. Then you'd have lots of people taking pictures, and you'd be bound to end up with some great ones! And I know Gabe would do a terrific job."

Grandpa Bill coughed. "A middle-school student as the wedding photographer?" he said. "Really?"

"Well, why not?" said John. "A middle-school

student designed and made the wedding dress, and the junior bridesmaid's gown. And even though Lulu refuses to tell me anything about them, I know she thinks they're both gorgeous!"

Zoey couldn't help feeling right then like she was very glad John was joining their family.

"After all," John continued, "we wanted a fun, low-stress, nontraditional wedding. We're certainly getting the nontraditional part."

"Let's do it!" Lulu said. She wiped her nose one last time. "Go call him, Zoey, and tell him we'd be *delighted* to have him shoot our wedding."

"We'll have to let him in on the secret . . . ," Zoey said, looking at her aunt for permission.

"Ack! The secret. I can't worry about *that* anymore. Just ask him to please not tell anyone except his parents and to please, please, pretty please, bring his camera and his talent tomorrow."

"I'll arrange it," John said. "You call him, Zoey, and then hand me the phone, okay?"

"Thank you, honey," Aunt Lulu said gratefully, looking at him like he was her personal wedding hero. Zoey noticed her grandparents exchange a look as well, one that said *they* really liked John too.

Zoey called Gabe, told him briefly about the plan, and wasn't surprised that he was beyond excited to do it. In fact, he kept thanking her over and over, until she handed the phone to John. John took the call in the kitchen, and the rest of the group waited in the living room, eating some crackers, until he returned.

"It's all settled," John said. "He didn't want us to pay him, but I insisted on at least a small fee for his time. He was just excited to get to start a professional portfolio by photographing a wedding. He did ask if he could bring an assistant to help with carrying cameras and lighting, which I said was fine."

Probably Josie, Zoey thought. *Oh well.*

"And you told him it had to remain a secret, right?" Zoey asked John.

"Yes," said John. "Though he did have to ask his parents for permission."

The family laughed, and Zoey felt enormously relieved. Everything was arranged, the wedding was tomorrow, and soon the secret would be out and the fun would begin. And, in the meantime, she had an evening of pasta and charades with the family to enjoy. After all, there was nothing left to go wrong!

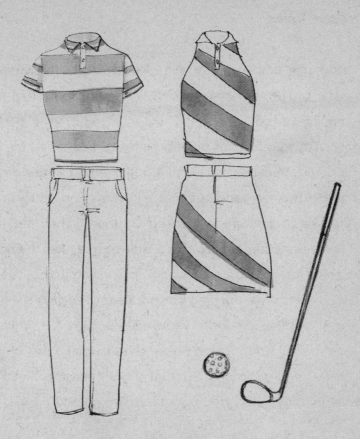

CHAPTER 10

Party! Party! Paaaaaarty!

The engagement party for my aunt is later today! I'm so, so, *sew* very excited! There's going to be food and friends and family there, and even though the weather is looking pretty rainy and gross, I just know it'll work out. I've got a great dress to wear, and I'm planning something fun with my hair, too. Now, if I can just make sure my brother and my dad wear what I tell them to, we'll be all set!

You may be confused about the golf outfit sketch I've posted, because this is *not* a golf-themed engagement party! But my grandparents are here visiting, so I wanted to sketch something inspired by them. They live in a retirement community with a golf course, and they play golf a lot, so I figured, why not look good doing it? Sew Zoey is really branching out this year (wedding dresses, golf outfits). I wonder what will be next . . . military uniforms? Hmm! I won't have time to make this before they head back to AZ, but I'll show them the sketch to see if they like it. Hoping for a hole in one!

The next day, Zoey, Marcus, and Mr. Webber left for Lulu's house mid morning. The party/wedding wouldn't be until the late afternoon, but they'd all planned to help John and Lulu with the setup and last-minute details. They would dress at Lulu's house just before the party. Zoey had showered at home, so that all she'd have to do later would be throw on her dress and maybe put on some pink lip gloss, if her father would allow it.

At Lulu's, there was already chaos. The steady drizzle outside was making the outdoor ceremony seem unlikely, and the tables and chairs couldn't be delivered until the rain stopped. And as the Webbers filed into the kitchen, hoping to be told what they could do to help, there was more bad news.

"The baker called," John said, with a nervous look at Lulu, who was drinking coffee and staring somewhat blankly at the countertop. "The bakery's basement flooded from all this rain, and that's where its ovens are. So they can't make the wedding cupcakes cake."

"It's just getting rather silly, isn't it?" Lulu said, with a small smile. "One thing after another. That's how weddings always are, really. I'd just hoped to avoid it with our small, surprise, *low-stress* version." She laughed. "Not low stress anymore."

John laughed too. "Agreed."

Mr. Webber spoke up. "I could run out to the grocery store and buy up a bunch of cupcakes, and we could arrange them like a cake? It's not perfect, but it could work."

Aunt Lulu nodded gratefully. "That would be wonderful. Thank you! That'll just leave us with where to have the ceremony if the rain doesn't stop."

Mr. Webber left for the store, and the rest of the family, including Zoey's grandparents, worked on weather contingency plans. When Mr. Webber returned with a large box, he placed it on the counter and said, somewhat regretfully, "This was the best I could find."

John and Lulu opened the box to find a selection of Halloween cupcakes. They were all orange and black, with cats and ghosts and witches on them. Lulu laughed again. "Oh my," she said. "This is really something. It'll have to do, I suppose. Halloween cupcakes at our wedding!"

"We didn't want traditional, right? At least the orange frosting kind of matches the color scheme," John said. He shrugged, as if cupcakes were the last thing on his mind.

But when Lulu's hairdresser came to do her

hair and makeup, and they disappeared into Lulu's room, John pulled Zoey, Mr. Webber, and Marcus into a huddle.

"Is there anything else we can do for wedding cake?" he asked. "Lulu was so excited about that cupcakes cake, and I really do want her to have her heart's desire today. She's already had to compromise on so much. I really wish *I* could bake!"

At the word "bake," Zoey thought immediately of Priti and her home ec class. Zoey did know someone who could bake—in fact, two people: Priti and her mom.

"Excuse me one second," she said to John, picking up her phone and running into the other room.

She called Priti and hurriedly explained about the party actually being a surprise wedding, and the lack of wedding cupcakes for the big event.

"I KNEW IT!" Priti screamed through the phone. "Zoey, I knew it. That is so awesome. And of course Mom and I can help. Let me think, though. . . . What could we make that would be ready by then and that won't need time for cooling and frosting?"

"Molten chocolate cakes?" Zoey suggested.

"MOLTEN CHOCOLATE CAKES!" Priti said. "Yes! I'll talk to my mom and call you back in one minute."

Zoey hung up the phone, waiting anxiously. Exactly one minute later, the phone rang, with Priti confirming that she and her mother were on their way to the store to get ingredients and that her mother had tons of ramekins from her old catering days to use for the cakes. They would make the batter at home and then bake the cakes at Lulu's, so they'd be warm and delicious for the reception.

"And of course we'll keep it all a *secret*," Priti said. "Though we might need extra sets of hands to get so many done in time. Can I call Kate and Libby?"

"YES! You're the best," Zoey said. She couldn't help feeling pleased by how all of her friends were coming through at the last minute to help her aunt have a wonderful wedding.

Zoey ran to report the good news to John, Marcus, and her father, who were delighted, and they all agreed to keep it a secret from Lulu.

"She'll love it," John said. "I'd like for the bride

to have a few *good* surprises on her wedding day. Now everyone had better get dressed!"

Remarkably, after Zoey's phone call to Priti, things took a turn for the better. The sun came out, and the tables and chairs were able to be set up outside. The ground was a bit soggy, but John was optimistic that the strong sun would soon dry it up. Lulu's hairdresser offered to style Zoey's hair and to secure the headband, so it wouldn't fall out when Zoey was dancing. She also applied just a touch of lip gloss and even a little mascara, which Mr. Webber had authorized. Zoey twirled in front of the mirror in her dress, feeling like she was ready to party.

Lulu wore a simple dark-blue wrap dress for the beginning of the party, but with her elegant hair and makeup, she looked stunning. She planned to change after the surprise announcement was made. As guests began arriving, congratulating John and Lulu on their engagement, Zoey's stomach began to feel jumpy. It was almost time. The secret they'd all held on to so dearly for weeks would be revealed! When all the guests had arrived, John gave

Grandma Dorothy a wink, which was the signal to begin.

Zoey's grandmother said to him loudly, so that everyone could hear, "So, John, have you two set a date yet?"

The guests were quiet, waiting for an answer. John looked at Lulu, wanting her to do the big reveal. Her cheeks immediately flushed, and she grinned from ear to ear, saying, "Actually, everyone, it's TODAY!"

Marcus, who had been ready and waiting with the guitar, strummed the beginning chords of "Going to the Chapel of Love."

There were gasps and a round of applause as everyone realized they would be attending a wedding that afternoon instead of an engagement party. Several people went up to John and Lulu and hugged them, wishing them well.

"I have to excuse myself now," Lulu said giddily, "to go and get dressed for my *wedding*!"

Zoey followed her aunt back to the bedroom. She had a very special gift to give her.

She helped her aunt into the gown, still

marveling at how well it fit her and how lovely the fabric was against her skin. Zoey pulled a small box from the bag she'd brought over and handed it to her aunt.

"What's this?" Lulu asked.

"A surprise," Zoey said. "Not from me, but from Daphne Shaw."

Aunt Lulu's eyes opened wide. "*Daphne Shaw* sent *me* a wedding gift?" She hurriedly tore off the ribbon and opened the box. There, resting on a piece of white velvet, was the beautiful blue garter.

"For your something blue," Zoey said. "You have something old, Grandma's earrings; something new, the dress; something borrowed, John's mother's bracelet; and now you have something blue!"

Lulu picked it up and examined it, seeing the small label on the inside. She smiled. Carefully, she slid the garter up one leg and then let her dress fall to conceal it. "It's absolutely perfect," she said. "I'd forgotten that saying, but somehow it all came together, didn't it?"

"Just like the wedding will," Zoey promised. "I'm

going to go out and help Dad, okay? You stay here and finish getting ready."

Lulu nodded. "Okay. And, Zoey," she said, pausing to look meaningfully at her niece, "this day wouldn't be nearly as special without you in it."

"Same," said Zoey, laughing a little. "Although, then we wouldn't have a bride, so it *really* wouldn't be special!"

Zoey headed back to the main part of the house, where Mr. Webber was directing guests outside. Rows of chairs had been set up to face a makeshift altar, which was a flower-covered arbor delivered by the florist that morning.

As Lulu was getting ready, Priti, Mrs. Holbrooke, Kate, and Mrs. Mackey had appeared, slipping into the kitchen to begin baking the cakes. They hadn't been able to get ahold of Libby, unfortunately, but they felt sure the four of them could get the baking done. Zoey told them the plan was to keep Lulu out of the kitchen, so the cakes would be a surprise.

"More secrets!" Kate said with an eye roll. "At least now I know why you missed tap class and roller-skating! Your dress is beautiful, by the way."

"Thanks!" said Zoey. She checked the clock and realized it was showtime. "I've got to head to the ceremony. See you!"

As Zoey and Sybil lined up to be part of the processional with Buttons, Mr. Webber gave Zoey a quick hug. "I'm heading up to the altar," he said. "I'll see you there."

"What?" asked Zoey. "Why?" Marcus was already up there with his guitar, to play the processional music, and John's best man was there as well, but Zoey had no idea why her father would be there.

"I'm the officiant," he said proudly. "I got certified online, and I'll be marrying the bride and groom. That's the favor Lulu asked me at our house a few weeks ago. Well, and she wanted to know if I was bringing a date."

"I was wondering that too!" Zoey told her dad.

"Well, she's out of town on business this weekend and couldn't cancel at the last minute," replied Mr. Webber. "But we've only gone out a few times. I'm not sure I'm ready to introduce her to you and Marcus, let alone the whole family!"

Zoey couldn't believe it. More secrets! But she was delighted her father would be leading the ceremony. It made it even more special. And she was getting used to the idea of him dating. Sort of.

Finally, it was time. Marcus began to play "Here Comes the Sun," and first, Zoey and then Sybil headed down the aisle. Zoey held Buttons's leash, and she looked quite stylish with her ring bearer pillow. Just before the ceremony, John had carefully placed the wedding bands into the little pocket on top, buttoned it, and gave Zoey—and Buttons—a hug.

Then Lulu appeared, looking like the most beautiful bride Zoey had ever seen. Zoey hadn't planned on crying at the wedding, but she couldn't help it. Lulu looked so happy, and so in love. She practically glowed.

Lulu glided down the aisle toward John. Marcus finished playing his song and put down his guitar, taking his place beside the best man. Mr. Webber welcomed everyone and began the ceremony.

Soon it was time for the rings. Zoey reached down to retrieve them from the pillow's pocket, but she could only find Lulu's and not John's. Zoey dug around with her fingers, then began searching the ground with her eyes, frantic.

Mr. Webber leaned over and whispered to Zoey, "What's wrong?"

"It's missing," she confessed, looking guiltily at Lulu and John, even though she had seen John put both rings into the pillow not fifteen minutes before. How could one have fallen out? "John's ring is gone! What are we going to do?"

Zoey's dad didn't miss a beat. "No matter—for now let's use mine, okay, John? Lulu?" Mr. Webber asked, slipping off the wedding ring he still wore on his right hand, despite having been a widower for so many years. "We'll search for the other one later."

Lulu clasped his hand gratefully and then took the ring her own sister had put on *her* husband's hand years ago.

The ceremony continued without incident, and finally, it was time to kiss the bride. Everyone cheered, with Zoey and Marcus cheering the loudest of all.

"Time to party!" Marcus said as the guests were led to their tables, which had been decorated with beautiful pink, orange, and red flowers. The food was from a local Thai restaurant, where John and Lulu had their first date, and everything was delicious. Zoey was seated at the bride's table, with her grandparents and her father and brother.

For the first time, Zoey noticed Gabe walking around, taking pictures. He'd been taking them the whole time, she supposed, but had been doing such a great job blending in with the guests and not being obvious. And, to her surprise, she knew his assistant, as well.

But it wasn't Josie.

"Libby!" Zoey hopped up to hug Libby, who was carrying some of Gabe's equipment, as well as gently reminding guests to please use the disposable cameras on the table. "I can't believe you're here! How did this happen?"

"Gabe asked me to be his assistant because we always talk about photography in our computer class." Libby beamed. "I was glad to, especially when I found out why you've been so busy lately. How did you make that wedding gown, Zoey? It's gorgeous! And your dress, too."

Zoey shrugged. "Thanks, Libby! I don't know, really, how I got the wedding dress done. It was such a blur! But Sean made my dress, actually, since I ran out of time. I'm just so glad Aunt Lulu is happy."

For their first dance as a married couple, the bride and groom danced the tango, as they'd planned, and Zoey couldn't help feeling proud of the gown she'd made. It showed off Lulu's beauty and moved very well on the dance floor.

"I'm going to go dance!" Zoey told Libby when it was time for others to join on the dance floor. "You come too, okay?"

"In a bit," Libby promised. "I'm working, you know!"

Zoey headed to the dance floor and danced her heart out. Most of the guests were dancing as well, so at times the dance floor was crowded, and there was some jostling and laughing as people bumped into one another. At one point Zoey found herself doing the twist next to her aunt, who was going down very low.

With a gasp, Zoey noticed that Lulu's dress actually had a seam that was opening up on one side. Zoey must have forgotten to use a lock stitch there, or had basted the seam but never properly sewn it.

Horrified by her mistake, Zoey grabbed Lulu's arm and whispered in her ear. She then led Lulu off the dance floor, through the grass, and toward the house. But the grass was still damp and slippery, and Zoey slid in her kitten heel, one toe landing on the hem of Lulu's dress and tearing it so that the bottom of the dress began to rip horizontally.

"Aunt Lulu, I'm so terribly sorry!" she shrieked. "I can't believe I just did that! And on your most important day." Zoey was near tears as she looked over the ragged hole in the dress, the rip in the seam, and the mud-covered hem. There was no way she could quickly stitch it all up, as she'd planned to do with the loose seam.

Aunt Lulu looked down at the rip and shrugged. "You know, Zoey, I know it's not perfect anymore, but this dress has done its duty, and it's not like I'll be wearing it again, right?" Aunt Lulu winked.

"Right!" Zoey said. "But what if it keeps ripping?"

"I have an idea," Lulu said. "But it's a little drastic."

"Okay," Zoey said. "You're the bride! Do what you need to do!"

With that, Lulu quickly tore at the fabric horizontally with her hands, bringing the hem of the dress to just below her knees.

"There," she said, with a nod. "Now I can *really* dance. And don't worry, Zoey—I'm having the time of my life, and I adore this dress. We are going to have fun all night long, and we're not going to worry about *anything*, okay?"

Zoey nodded, amazed by her aunt's ability to turn lemons into lemonade. The two of them returned to the dance floor to show off Aunt Lulu's new "reception dress." The group cheered, and Zoey couldn't help cheering along with them. What a woman her aunt was.

When it was time for the desserts to be brought out, Zoey overheard Aunt Lulu joking to someone about the Halloween cupcakes. Zoey couldn't wait to see her face when the real desserts appeared.

Priti, Kate, and their moms came out, all wearing professional white aprons, provided by Mrs. Holbrooke, and began delivering the beautiful molten chocolate cakes to each seat. They'd even made a special large one, shaped like a heart, which had "Lulu and John" written with gold edible glitter in the pink frosting.

Lulu was so surprised and delighted, she burst into tears and hugged each of Zoey's friends, thanking them for stepping in at the last moment to help. Zoey hugged them also, and she was grateful she knew so many amazing and talented people.

The cakes were delicious! All the guests loved them, and Zoey knew they'd be a hit at the party. Zoey would definitely need to thank Mrs. Holmes on Monday for teaching them such a delicious recipe.

When the wedding was finally over, and the guests had left, Zoey, Marcus, and Mr. Webber got ready to leave. They packed up their things and kissed the bride good-bye.

"Thank you for all you did for us today," John said. "Lulu and I will never forget it."

"We won't either!" Marcus assured him. "What a day! What a party!"

"Have a wonderful honeymoon, Aunt Lulu and *Uncle* John," Zoey said with a giggle. "I hope it goes smoother than the wedding planning!"

"I don't," John said knowingly. "Sometimes the sweetest moments are found in the middle of the biggest messes."

"Isn't that the truth," said Mr. Webber. "I'd say that's family in a nutshell. Welcome to ours, John."

CHAPTER 11

Back to Reality!

I can't believe it's over. I really can't! Yesterday my favorite aunt got *married* (yes, that's right! It wasn't an engagement party—it was a surprise wedding. Did any of you guess?), and she wore the wedding gown I've posted here. I'd been sewing it for about three weeks straight to get it ready in time. And even though I thought I'd done my best, I managed to leave a seam in the skirt unsewn (it was basted, but not properly sewn up), and the skirt ended up ripping on the dance floor. Then there was a separate mishap, and Lulu ended up having to tear off the bottom part of the skirt and rock it as a knee-length reception dress! Luckily, she's so awesome, she made it look cool, but as the designer (and niece and junior bridesmaid), I can't help feeling like I let her down. It's not a very good feeling. . . . But I know she loved the dress, so I'm happy!

And—get this!—my new uncle John's wedding ring is missing! It fell out the ring pillow somewhere in the backyard, and we searched and searched, but we still can't find it. Superstitious readers—that doesn't mean anything, does it?

Monday morning felt very ordinary to Zoey, with no wedding dress to work on or wedding to help plan. She packed her lunch and headed off to school, like always. As she was getting books from her locker, she heard her phone beep and then saw the following text:

> **Having the most marvelous time on our honeymoon. Thank you for my dreamy dress and for being a dream of a niece! Xoxoxo**

There was also a picture of Lulu and John in front of a palm tree, holding hands. Zoey couldn't help grinning from ear to ear as she tucked her phone into her backpack and headed off toward home ec class. Yes, she'd made a mistake on her aunt's dress, but Lulu was happy, and that was the most important thing. And, truthfully, Zoey had learned a very important lesson from the experience, which was to always *triple-check* her seams!

When Zoey arrived in class and plopped down next to Priti, she realized with a start that it was the day of the apron innovation contest. Zoey had completely forgotten! She'd meant to bring her apron home over the weekend and work on it Sunday, after the wedding, but she'd been so excited Friday that she hadn't put it in her bag, and never gave it a second thought.

"Oh my gosh, I completely forgot the apron contest," she whispered to Priti.

Priti had her apron out and ready, and it was starched and pressed. "Well, it's no wonder," she said. "You've been a *little* bit busy! Don't worry—I'm sure yours is great."

Zoey wasn't so sure. She hurriedly grabbed it from her cubby in the room and shook it out over her table to examine it. Looking at it critically for the first time, Zoey was embarrassed to see how sloppy the hem was, and some obvious chalk marks from marking it were showing. She had added some minor innovation, by using snaps in the back instead of making it a tie, because Zoey always had trouble tying things behind her own back. But it was nowhere near as good as it should have been. It wasn't what other students would expect from her, and it wasn't what she expected of herself.

"I really messed up," she confessed to Priti. "I kind of thought I was such an experienced sewer that I could just throw this together, and maybe even win, but I was too distracted and I never put in any effort. And it shows."

She sighed heavily. It felt awful to have to show something she wasn't proud of. Especially when everyone in the class expected her to have something really neat. Zoey felt like she was learning another big lesson—to give everything her best effort every time and that nothing is guaranteed.

"Don't worry, Zoey," Priti said kindly. "Some kids didn't even finish theirs. And you were busy working on an actual wedding gown! It's not like you were goofing off."

"Still," said Zoey, "I could have done better."

One by one the kids in home ec got up to present their aprons. Zoey gamely tried to present hers, showing the snaps and whatnot, but she noticed Mrs. Holmes look slightly disappointed.

When Sean got up to show his apron, Zoey couldn't help being impressed. His apron was really well made and was definitely innovative. He'd taken wax and covered the cotton all over, so that the fabric would be somewhat spill proof, and he'd also added a five-by-seven inch pocket for recipe cards *and* made the sides extra wide, so that they would wrap around to the back and cover more of the wearer's clothes. The neck and waist straps were extra wide too, which made the apron look more comfortable to wear. It was a really neat-looking design.

Zoey clapped loudly for Sean when he was done presenting, as did the rest of the class, even Carter. Some of the kids may have initially thought it was odd that Sean was so good at sewing, but he'd turned out to be *so* good at it, they'd forgotten they ever thought it was weird and now just seemed impressed.

When Sean won the award for best apron, Zoey got up and went over to congratulate him.

"Great job, Sean," she said. "You really made a cool apron! And I love the wax trick. I might try that myself."

Sean looked flattered and pleased by all the attention. "Thanks, Zoey," he said. "It means a lot to me."

"I hope we can start that club together," Zoey

said. She couldn't believe now that she'd ever felt threatened by Sean. He'd helped her make her beautiful junior bridesmaid's dress, and now she had a new friend who loved to do the same thing she did. She didn't need to feel envious of him! If anything, a little friendly competition in home ec class might make it more fun. She hadn't done well in the apron contest, but she would definitely bring it on the next project. Sew Zoey would show everyone her true colors!

"Too bad your little snaps didn't help your apron win," Ivy said on her way back to her desk. "Your hem was uneven, by the way." She and Bree snickered to each other, their unimaginative but well-sewn aprons folded over their arms.

Before Zoey could reply, Sean cut in. "Zoey was a *little* busy the past few weeks designing and sewing a custom-made wedding gown," he said. "And by the way, whenever you guys talk badly about her, you just make yourselves look jealous and catty."

"That's what you think," Ivy snapped, but she and Bree moved on quickly, without further comment.

Zoey looked at Sean gratefully. "Thanks," she said.

"Friends?" he said, as if it were a question. He put out his fist, which she quickly bumped with hers.

"Friends," she answered.

A week flew by, and before Zoey knew it, her grandparents had flown back to Arizona, and Aunt Lulu and Uncle John had returned from their honeymoon. They invited Zoey and her friends, and their moms who had helped with the wedding, over to their house for brunch, to thank them all for pitching in at the last minute and making the event a success.

Zoey couldn't wait to see her aunt and uncle. She still wasn't used to thinking of Lulu and John as her "aunt and *uncle*" yet! But she felt sure that it would become a habit very quickly. John had proven himself to be almost as wonderful as Lulu during all the hectic wedding planning and crises.

John and Lulu had arranged the brunch—which included delicious frittata, fruit, and bacon—out on their back patio. The Webbers arrived first, and Zoey couldn't believe how tan and happy Lulu and John looked.

"Zoey!" Lulu cried, giving her an enormous hug. "Can you believe it's all over? Just a few weeks ago, I took you for cupcakes and told you the news. And now I'm a happily married woman." She smiled dazzlingly over at John, who returned the look.

"I *can't* believe it," Zoey said. "It feels like it was only a few days ago, but so much has happened!"

The guests arrived almost all at once, as the Holbrookes had given Sean a ride, Gabe's parents had picked up Libby, and the Mackeys lived close-by. Zoey was happy to see all her friends on a Sunday morning and happier still that she didn't have to lie to them anymore.

As the kids were all sitting together in a circle, with the adults off to the side in their own circle, Zoey said, "You guys don't know what a relief it is to have the wedding over and not have to hide the wedding gown from you anymore!"

Kate laughed uncharacteristically loudly for her. "*You* don't know what a relief it is to not have to hear your ridiculous excuses anymore!"

Libby quickly nodded and chimed in, "Seriously! You were doing 'engagement dresses,' then 'Etsy orders,' then you were doing the wedding dress 'early, in case Lulu changed her mind'. . ."

Priti and Gabe started laughing as well. "You were a mess, Zoey," Priti said. "You even flubbed your apron project in home ec. *But*," she said, stressing the word, "I don't know another person in the world who would work so hard to help their aunt throw her dream wedding in her dream dress in just a few weeks. You are one terrific friend, Zoey Webber." And she held up her glass of orange juice to toast her.

Zoey's other friends did the same, and they clinked glasses and cheered. Zoey couldn't help blushing and feeling like she really didn't deserve *quite* so much praise. After all, Sean had sewn her junior bridesmaid's dress for her, and the wedding gown had ripped! But the wedding had been a success, and the whole family was happy, so maybe that was enough. Maybe the perfect wedding never really *is* perfect.

"Oh my gosh!" Priti cried. She leaned down and picked up something beside her chair. "Look at this!"

Everyone looked over, and when Lulu saw what was in Priti's hand, she yelled "Eureka!"

John jumped up, ran over to Priti, and took the object from her hand. "I can't thank you enough," he said, clasping Priti's hand.

It was his wedding ring. Somehow it had slipped out of the pillow pocket, or Buttons had jiggled it out, and it had been sitting on the muddy lawn—half buried—since the wedding.

"Don't thank me!" Priti said, somewhat embarrassed. "If I were better at sewing, it might have stayed in the pocket."

John shook his head. "But then we wouldn't have this wonderful story to tell for the rest of our lives." He beamed at Zoey and her friends. "I'm sure it's not your fault, but, you know, it's the mistakes, and the mishaps, that make our lives full and funny and interesting."

Zoey couldn't help giggling. "Then my life is *very* full and *very* interesting!"

All her friends laughed. "It sure is," Libby agreed. "And we wouldn't have it any other way."

Lulu stood up and came over to John, who was using a napkin dipped in water to clean up the ring a little. She took it from him gently, then holding his left hand, slipped it onto his ring finger, which had been bare since their ceremony.

"With this ring, I thee wed," she said tenderly. They kissed, and the entire group cheered again, just as everyone had at the ceremony.

Zoey really felt like she might burst with joy— everything had come together in the end, despite a few rips in the seams.

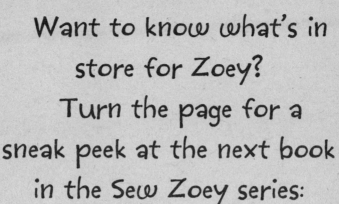

Want to know what's in store for Zoey?
Turn the page for a sneak peek at the next book in the Sew Zoey series:

CLOTHES MINDED

Nutty for Knitting!

Hello, readers! Your friend Zoey is suffering from a big dose of *reality* at the moment. Everything seems so calm and almost boring after the flurry of planning Aunt Lulu's surprise wedding (in only three weeks). Now that the wedding is over, it's like I've forgotten what normal life is like with just school, homework, friends, designing, sewing, and my blog. . . . Oh, yeah—I'm actually still pretty busy! ☺

Anyway, I've always wanted to learn to knit, so I just started teaching myself with a book Aunt Lulu gave me. I've already tried to make a few things, including the scarf in this sketch. My next project might be mittens with different-colored thumbs, but I've heard that gloves and mittens are very difficult. Do any of you knit? If so, please post your helpful tips in the comments! And stay tuned for the (hopefully cozy) results of my knitting projects. . . .

Monday mornings were difficult for Zoey Webber. Not because she had a hard time waking up (although she did), and not because she disliked school (she liked it very much), but because her weekends were always so much fun. She spent time with her friends, made pancakes with her father and older brother, and spent hours and hours working on new sketches and designs for her Sew Zoey label.

So even though Zoey was pleased with her Monday morning outfit, which included a skirt made from the top of an old pair of her brother's jeans that she'd stitched to a length of green floral fabric, she found herself sitting in home ec with her chin propped up on her hands, feeling like she was in a bit of a postweekend slump.

One of her best friends, Priti Holbrooke—whose recent penchant for dark, goth clothes was at odds with her loud, sunny personality—breezed into the room. She complimented Zoey's outfit before plopping down beside her and pulling out her phone to send a text message. Seconds later, Sean Waschikowski, a relatively new friend of Zoey's, plopped down on her other side, even though his assigned seat was across the room.

The bell for class to begin was about to ring.

"Hi, Priti. Hi, Sean," Zoey said, her chin still in her hands. She couldn't help wishing she'd been able to sleep in that morning. Even though it was only early fall, the cooler mornings made her want to stay in bed longer.

"You look glum, chum," Sean said.

"I'm not!" Zoey protested. "Honestly. It's just Monday mornings. . . . You know. The weekend's over."

Priti nodded sympathetically, slipping her phone into her backpack. "I *do* know," she said. "I've got to switch all my stuff over to my dad's place tonight, because I spent the weekend at my mom's. Ugh."

"I know what you *both* need to cheer up," Sean said, raising his eyebrows and wiggling them. "An inspiring new project!"

Zoey's ears immediately perked up, and with them, her mood. "What do you have in mind?" she asked.

"C'mon, you remember," he said playfully. "I sewed your junior bridesmaid's dress for your aunt's wedding, and you promised you'd owe me one, and then I said we should start a . . ."

"Fashion club!" Zoey finished for him. "That's right; I remember."

Sean drummed his fingers on Zoey's desk. "You got it. My cousin Tessa has one at her high school. Her club is sponsored by their local fashion design college. Most design colleges don't offer sponsorships to middle schools, but I thought we could start the club ourselves here at Mapleton Prep."

"What a cool idea!" Priti responded. "But what is it? A club of fashionable people?"

Zoey shrugged. "I don't know either! Sean, what exactly would the club *do*?"

Sean grinned. "Whatever we want! We'd make it an official club, like the chess club or the musical theater club. And then we'd have to find members, but they don't have to be just designers—fashion clubs are for anyone with an interest in fashion. The people in my cousin's club want to be interior designers, fashion merchandisers, set designers, costumer designers, graphic designers—you name it."

"Then why is it called a fashion club?" Priti asked.

Sean shook his head. "I don't know; I guess that's just how it got started. Or maybe because most of the activities are focused on clothing."

"I don't know anything about starting a club," Zoey said. "I'm not even *in* any clubs at school!"

"But I am—I'm in the musical theater club," Sean replied. "And my cousin can fill us in on how her fashion club works to get us started."

"Hmm." Zoey still wasn't sure. She doubted starting a new club was as easy as Sean was making it sound.

"Go on, Zoey," urged Priti. "You know you'll love it if you do it. You'll have more people to talk with about your work! You know I never understand when you try to explain your projects to me."

"That's not true," Zoey said. "And you're learning to sew. You made Buttons's ring-bearer pillow for Aunt Lulu's wedding!"

Priti snorted. "And we all know how *that* turned out," she said, referring to Zoey's new uncle's wedding band falling out of the pillow's pocket and getting lost during the ceremony. Uncle John used Mr. Webber's wedding band for the ceremony, and they didn't find the original wedding band until after the honeymoon.

"But the pillow *looked* great," Zoey said loyally. "And it's not like Buttons understood she wasn't supposed to move around very much! She did her doggie best."

"Do the club," Priti said, refusing to let Zoey change the subject.

"I'll do most of the work, Zoey," Sean pleaded as their home ec teacher, Mrs. Holmes, stood from her desk to begin class. "Please? I just need you for talent and ideas and fashion support!"

Zoey looked back and forth between her old friend and new one, both of whom seemed positive the fashion club and Zoey Webber were destined to be together.

"Oh, all right," Zoey agreed and then grinned. "Let's do it, Sean. I do need something new to work on, and my knitting isn't going as well as I'd hoped."

"I can help with that," Sean whispered as he stood up to head to his seat. "My grandmother taught me to knit. But don't tell anyone—it's hard enough for guys at this school to accept that I sew!"

Zoey agreed to meet Sean at school on Tuesday morning to start working on his idea. Sean had made an appointment for them to meet with the principal, Ms. Austen, before homeroom to find out if it was even possible for them to start a new club.

Zoey's brother, Marcus, dropped her off early, so early that the school was eerily silent, and many of the classrooms didn't have their lights on yet. She felt like she had to tiptoe and speak softly in the hallways. She was relieved when she caught up with Sean by his locker and was no longer by herself. Together, they walked to the principal's office.

"You ready?" he asked Zoey. She nodded, not wanting to say out loud that she actually had a few butterflies in her stomach. Even though Zoey had a great relationship with Ms. Austen, who was an admirer of Zoey's designs and blog, Ms. Austen was still the principal, and talking to the principal always felt like a big deal.

Sean knocked boldly on Ms. Austen's door.

"Come in!" Ms. Austen said, opening it and ushering them toward the chairs facing her desk.

Sean and Zoey sat down, and Zoey watched as Ms. Austen opened her travel cup of coffee, stirred in a packet of sugar, and took a careful sip. "Mmm," she said. "I've never been a morning person. Coffee helps."

"Now," she continued, "I'm assuming two of my most ambitious students are here early on a Tuesday morning for a very good reason. How can I help you?"

Sean cleared his throat. "Well, Zoey and I would like to start a fashion club. We want it to be an official club, with a regular meeting day, and field trips and everything, and its focus would be on encouraging students with an interest in all types of design, from clothing to interior to graphic."

Zoey and Sean had talked on the phone the night before, and he'd rehearsed what he was going to say. Zoey thought it sounded great.

Evidently, Ms. Austen did too, because she sat back in her chair, nodding and looking quite pleased. Zoey noticed Ms. Austen was wearing a beautiful vintage Diane von Furstenberg wrap dress and bright blue T-strapped heels that day. If anyone would be sympathetic to their cause, it would be her.

"What a great idea!" Ms. Austen said. "I love to give my students opportunities to explore their passions, especially ones that aren't necessarily addressed in our standard curriculum, although home ec is a start. However, there are a few things we need to consider."

Zoey bit her lip. That sounded serious. "Like what?"

Ms. Austen rocked back and forth in her chair, tenting her fingertips. "The school year is well underway, so the school's budget for clubs has already been divided among the existing clubs."

Sean nodded. "Right, okay."

Zoey hadn't even thought about the club needing a budget. But she supposed that field trips and materials and whatever else they might need would cost money.

"So you'll have to charge dues to your members," Ms. Austen explained. "And you'll need to choose a president for the club, advertise to get members, decide what your dues will be and collect them, choose a meeting day, and so on."

Zoey had her sketchbook with her, as always, and whipped it out to jot down notes.

"And lastly," said Ms. Austen, "you'll need to come up with a plan for meeting activities and find a teacher who will be willing to act as your club's leader and supervisor."

To Zoey, the list was already starting to sound like a bit more than she'd anticipated. But Sean was leaning forward in his seat, a huge smile on his face.

"That's it? Great!" he said. "So you're fine with us getting started right away?"

Ms. Austen nodded. "Absolutely. I'd be very proud for our middle school to be the first in the area to have a fashion club!"

Zoey and Sean exchanged a look. She couldn't help feeling bolstered by the principal's enthusiasm. It would be neat to do something totally unique at Mapleton Prep. After all, it wasn't the first time Zoey had done something most twelve-year-olds hadn't! (Including being a judge on the TV show *Fashion Showdown*, making a wedding dress, and having a famous Hollywood starlet wear one of her designs.) Starting a club would seem like a piece of cake compared to those things.

A bell rang, signaling that students had three minutes to make it to homeroom. Zoey and Sean gathered up their books to leave.

"Keep me posted," Ms. Austen said. "And thank you for setting such a good example for your fellow students."

Sean and Zoey left the office, moving swiftly in the direction of their homerooms.

"That went great!" Sean said. "This'll be easy."

"Easy?" Zoey repeated. "Ha! We have a lot to do. But I was thinking maybe Mrs. Holmes from home ec might be willing to be our club leader. I can ask her later if you want."

Sean nodded. "I knew I could count on you, Webber!"

Zoey laughed. "We're a good team, Waschi— um . . ."

"Waschi*kowski*. It's a bit of a mouthful, I know," Sean said, shrugging. "But we really are a good team. Fashion club here we come!"

For a Great *Prints*ipal!

Guess *what*? I've found a new project—but not the kind I usually do. My terrific friend S. and I are starting a fashion club at our middle school! It's going to be so cool. We got permission from our school's principal, and our home ec teacher has agreed to be our club leader (and was *sew* nice about it! Thanks, Mrs. H!)

I've never done anything like this before, but S is in the musical theater club, so he knows what he's doing. Plus, he seems to be really good at convincing people to do things he wants. (Ahem . . . like getting me to help him start the club!)

In honor of our school's wonderful, fashionista principal, I've sketched this outfit, which I know would look really great on her. It's got a slight vintage feel, which is her style, but the prints make it modern. Maybe we'll even make it for her as a project in the club!

Zoey sat in her school's auditorium Thursday morning, surrounded by her girlfriends. Ms. Austen had called an all-school assembly, and Zoey and her friends Priti, Kate Mackey, and Libby

Flynn, as well as the rest of the student body at Mapleton Prep, were wondering why.

"Maybe they're giving us an extra-long winter break this year?" Priti said hopefully. "Or getting rid of report cards?"

The rest of the girls laughed. Kate, who was devoted to sports, said, "Maybe she's announcing the soccer team's status in the state championships."

Libby shook her head. "You guys, it's probably just some assembly about a famous scientist or something."

But Zoey didn't think any of those suggestions were right. She could tell by the way Ms. Austen stood at the podium, nervously flipping through papers and tucking her hair behind her ears. The principal had something important to tell them. And Zoey couldn't wait to hear what it was.